I0667999

Wet, Wild and Willing

The sexcapades of a single man

First Edition

Published by The Nazca Plains Corporation
Las Vegas, Nevada
2008

ISBN: 978-1-934625-85-9

Published by

The Nazca Plains Corporation ®
4640 Paradise Rd, Suite 141
Las Vegas NV 89109-8000

PUBLISHER'S NOTE
Wet, Wild and Willing is a work of fiction created wholly by *Lew Bull's* imagination. All characters are fictional and any resemblance to any persons living or deceased is purely by accident. No portion of this book reflects any real person or events.

Cover, Fleshblack
Art Director, Blake Stephens

DEDICATION

To Tony and Mark,
Good friends are hard to find –
True friends, even harder.
Thank you for your care and support.

Wet, Wild and Willing

The sexcapades of a single man

First Edition

Lew Bull

TABLE OF CONTENTS

HOME

Mike was an ardent fan of the Irish dramatist and novelist, Oscar Wilde. Not that he enjoyed reading his works, so much as reading his quirky sayings and quips. And it was two of these that formed the backbone to Mike's possible existence. The first saying that Mike enjoyed was Wilde's quote from his play *Lady Windermere's Fan* which said, 'I can resist anything but temptation' and the second was from *The Portrait of Dorian Gray* which said, 'I like persons better than principles, and I like persons with no principles better than anything else in the world'.

Mike had always had a penchant for the good life to the extent of 'misbehaving' himself as much as possible, and he seemed to attract like-minded people, that is, the people with no principles. I say 'misbehaving', because to Mike, his behavior was anything but good – good for him and hopefully good for the other person. Mike always liked to please in everything that he did.

Mike was a happy-go-lucky sort of guy who was young and liked adventure, by this I mean he liked going to places of interest both from a historical as well as a sexual nature. The historical aspect led him to cities around the USA and the sexual nature enticed him to what those cities had to offer. However, it had been for quite some time that Mike had thought of possibly flying overseas to see what the rest of the world had to offer both historically and sexually.

Mike wasn't in any type of relationship, principled or otherwise, and although he had many friends, he tended to be a loner, only in the sense that he enjoyed doing things on his own. So when it came to planning his holidays, he always planned around himself and his desires. After years of contemplation, this particular year he had decided to spread his wings to further climes and go off to Europe in the hopes of tasting the unprincipled life to be found around the big cities of Europe.

His friends who knew his ways, laughed when he said that he'd decided to have a taste of something European.

"What's wrong with the guys here?" his friends had asked.

To which he'd replied that there was nothing wrong with American men, it's just that he felt he needed the taste of something Mediterranean that he had always longed for.

"Just think of the hunky, olive-skinned, lean Italians or those romantically seductive French men," he had told those same friends, making them wish they were also planning on heading to Europe. "And I hear that Czech boys are hung like horses!"

"Do you think American's aren't also hung like horses?" retorted a friend.

Mike was well aware that his friend was right in what he said, but it was a taste of the 'other side of life' that he wanted. He knew all about American boys and men, and their desires and physical attributes, which he had enjoyed enormously, but now he wanted to explore the beds of Europe.

Mike had saved up his money for his first trip overseas and was excited at the prospect of visiting foreign cities and meeting new people. It was not that he had a disliking for the locals, but the urge to taste life outside of the States was getting to him. He'd watched various television travel programs dealing with places in Europe and his appetite had been whetted.

He had spent the past year working hard as a construction worker, saving up in order to go for a well-deserved holiday. He had, in the past, often gone on a holiday to the coast or to visit relatives, but this time he had decided to venture further afield and taste life in other countries, and had decided to tour around Europe.

Friends and family had encouraged him to take the trip but had jokingly warned him of the vices that he might encounter on his travels.

"Like what?" he had enquired, innocently.

"Oh you never know," replied his caring sister. "You might find some strange women in an equally strange place so you'd better look after yourself."

Mike chuckled at her comment, as he knew he had no fears of finding 'some strange women' as his caring sister had said. If anything he was hoping instead to find some strange men! Maybe even come back home with a rugged Italian or French boyfriend! After all, he sensed it was getting time for him to find someone and settle down.

Mike, being a construction worker, was muscular from the hard labor, and well tanned from often working shirtless in the sun. He was 28, had short sun-bleached blonde hair and a radiant smile, broad shoulders and chest, slim waist, big hands, arms and legs. Physically, he had everything going for him, including being well-hung, according to many, and could quite easily attract a boyfriend, if he so desired, thanks to his overall package. In fact, many of his friends had wondered why he didn't already have someone in his life, but that was his choice. Mike was an easy-going, fun-loving guy who enjoyed life to the full and really was happy to play the field, so to say.

Mike had realized his sexual preferences at an early age and had come out of the closet, so to speak, to his family and friends and they had all, at some time, tried to match him up with someone, but Mike had been fussy and turned down all his potential suitors. It wasn't that he was fussy in the sense that he was critical of people's flaws, it's just that he felt he wasn't ready to go into a steady relationship. Mike still had a lot of wild oats to sow before he was ready for 'married life,' be it with whomever, and this meant that he was happy to go and mingle with the Europeans around Europe while he sorted out his desires in life.

"Would you really bring home an Italian or French boyfriend?" his sister had cautiously once asked.

"Maybe!" was the assertive response. "Why not?"

"But you can't speak either language, Mike," she had whined.

"You don't have to know a language to make love," was his philosophical answer. "And in any case, we have plenty of Italians and French living in the States, so learning the language wouldn't be a problem."

Mike seemed to have an answer for everything.

In planning his trip, Mike went from one travel agent to another, collecting brochures of various cities that interested him, until he had enough to probably open up his own travel agency. The brochures were studied, the suitcase was eventually packed, and the air tickets purchased. Mike was ready for the holiday of his life. He would be going during the summer, so it would be warm and therefore, clothing would be kept to a minimum, much to his relief, as Mike was not one for dressing up if he didn't have to. If he was offered the opportunity, Mike would probably be quite content to walk the streets in a pair of shorts or cut off jeans and a vest. It was thanks to his love of the outdoors that Mike was happy to bear himself to the elements.

In planning his holiday, he had decided to visit selected cities rather than go on an organized tour with a group of people. Admittedly being with a group might have allowed him contact with people probably his own age, but by going on his own, meant he would be free to mingle with the locals and go where he wanted to, rather than being ushered around as part of a group and restricted to doing certain things.

Mike's nephew, nineteen-year-old Barry, had nagged him about going overseas and had said that he wanted to accompany his uncle, but Mike wasn't sure that he wanted a hormone-driven teenager accompanying him, when he himself was hoping to allow his own hormones some freedom.

"I won't cramp your style, Uncle Mike," said Barry, fluttering his eyelids in an effort to win favor with his only uncle.

"Meaning what, young man?" enquired Mike.

"Well, if you want to go out on your own, I won't stop you."

Mike burst out laughing at the audacity of a teenager giving him permission to go out on his own. He had a mind of his own and didn't need anyone to say when he could or could not go out. What did concern him was that if they traveled together, they'd probably end up sharing a room together and what if he met someone and wanted to bring the person back to his hotel.

He really liked Barry and although Barry was aware of his uncle's sexuality, Mike didn't want to flaunt it in the young man's face. On the other hand, he thought it might be fun to have Barry along with him, but in small doses.

"I'll pay for him to go," said Mike's sister, Barry's mother.

This placed extra influence on Mike, who was toying with the idea of allowing his nephew to accompany him on his holiday, now that it had been broached.

"I'll tell you what, why don't you come over later and join me in Berlin or somewhere like that, then at least you get to have a short holiday?"

Barry at first rejected the idea out of hand, but when both his mother and Mike explained that he still had college to attend, he agreed that a shorter holiday would be better than no holiday at all. And so, with excitement in the air, uncle and nephew set about to study the brochures in more depth.

After having browsed through the brochures, Mike decided to focus his interests in London, Amsterdam, Paris, Berlin, and Rome, before heading home again. From his selection of cities, it became apparent that he was determined to have a sexually stimulating holiday as most of these cities had reputations of being havens for sexual fun, and that was what he was after. It was decided that Barry would join Mike in Berlin in Germany and travel with his uncle until they returned to the States together.

***

The American Airlines plane lifted off gently from the runway at JFK airport and headed out over the Atlantic Ocean in an Easterly direction, bound for London, England. Mike settled back in his seat and picked up one of the airline magazines in the pocket in front of him and glanced at the pictures. The crew, in the meantime, was busily passing around drinks and preparing for the dinner service. Mike noticed one of the flight stewards, a young man of approximately his own age, who always smiled broadly every time he passed by Mike. Mike chose to smile back and very soon they were in conversation. Mike had no one sitting beside him on the plane, so he felt he was able to speak freely to the steward without a nearby passenger listening in to their conversation, and found out that the young man's name was Clint. Throughout the flight, Clint made it his business to ply Mike with drinks, not for the intention of getting him drunk, but rather to be able to make contact with him on a regular basis.

After dinner had been served and trays had been removed, most of the passengers settled down to sleep, but Mike sat watching the various movies on his screen. Once most of the lights had been dimmed, Mike switched off his individual TV set and settled down to sleep, but was constantly aware of crew and the odd passengers walking past his seat. He sat in the dim light with his eyes open, watching the various people and then Clint came by.

"Problem sleeping?" he asked as he came to a halt next to Mike's seat.

"You could say that."

"Do you want to come to the back of the plane? We're pretty much finished what we have to do so I'll have time to talk to you, if you'd like."

Mike realized that he wasn't going to get much sleep, so he took up Clint's offer and went to the back of the plane where some of the other crew was sitting chatting.

"Where are you headed?" enquired Clint, still smiling sweetly and broadly at Mike.

"Obviously off to London, then on to Europe."

"That sounds great. Holiday or business?"

"Holiday," replied Mike.

"Have you ever been to London before?"

Mike laughed.

"No, this is my first trip out of the country."

"Oh!" said a surprised Clint. "Are you going to relatives?"

Again Mike smiled, knowing that his intention was to do all the things he'd not done or been allowed to do back home, so relatives, even if he'd had some there, would be out of the question.

"No family or relatives. I'm off to have a good time," he replied with a twinkle in his eye.

Clint understood Mike's message and winked back knowingly.

"It's great to get away from family and misbehave. That's why I became a flight steward."

"Do you meet many people on your flights?"

"All the time," Clint replied, "and sometimes it leads to a good time as well."

Mike wasn't sure whether Clint was suggesting something in particular to him by that last statement, but he felt that nothing could happen between them on the plane with so many people around.

"Do you know anyone in London?" asked Clint.

"Not a soul," replied Mike.

"I have a friend who works in a shop in London, if you'd like to meet him," continued Clint.

"Thanks that would be nice. I suppose it could be lonely in a strange place. What sort of shop does he work in and where is it?"

Clint hesitated before answering.

"I'll write down his address for you."

He went to find a note pad, then wrote down the details and handed it to Mike.

"Thanks, Clint," said Mike, looking at the address. "Is this in the center of London?"

"Yep! No trouble to get there and I think you might like him. Just tell him I sent you."

"What's his name and what's he like?" enquired Mike.

"His name's Mitch and the only way I can describe him is he's big, but I think you two would get on well."

With that, Clint's face beamed as he described his friend. Mike sat listening to the description of Clint's friend, so much so, that he began to become interested in meeting this 'big' man.

"He sounds fascinating," remarked Mike.

"He is, but I'm sure you'll still have a good time in London, what with your good looks and strong body," said Clint, eyeing Mike's broad shoulders and trim waist.

Mike blushed.

"You don't have to feel embarrassed," remarked Clint. "I mean what I say; you've got everything going for you – tight ass, big package..."

Mike looked down at his crotch when Clint said this, and noticed that his package, as the young air steward had said, had grown since talking to Clint. Maybe it was the thoughts of Clint's 'big' friend that was sending Mike's hormones on a quick spin.

After spending some time with Clint and the others at the back of the plane, Mike began to feel tired.

The rest of the flight was uneventful with Mike returning to his seat and eventually managing to fall asleep. In the early hours of the following morning, after breakfast had been delivered to all the passengers, the gray skies of England greeted the flight.

A light drizzle covered Heathrow Airport, but that was not about to dampen Mike's excitement at the start of his journey around Europe. He thanked Clint for the flight and the details, said farewell and said that he hoped they might bump into each other in London and that he would definitely look up Clint's friend, and then he departed.

Mike made his way through customs and headed for the underground to catch the train into the center of London.

A Boner Book

LONDON

By the time that Mike reached his hotel in the Bayswater area, London was awake and buzzing. The traffic was busy and the people were hurrying from place to place amidst the drizzle that kept falling. Mike booked into his hotel, which was very simply furnished, dumped his suitcase and then headed off to see the sights of London. His dilemma was what to do first.

He headed off towards the Thames and the London Eye, where he stood and admired both the huge wheel and the fast flowing river and its passing traffic, and then by mid-morning, caught the underground train to find Clint's friend's shop. Mike followed Clint's instructions and finally arrived at the front door of the shop. Mike looked up at the sign and his mind began to wonder. He had ventured into a leather shop; and it wasn't a furnishing shop!

It's amazing how the leather scene spans age groups and it's the one area in which older guys are accepted openly. Mike had only once got involved in a leather scene, not because he had reached a stage in his life where he couldn't pick up guys, but rather, he'd always taken a liking for the feel and smell of leather; the tight leather clothing worn by the guys and the sexuality associated with leather. He wasn't interested in the S & M scene and was more focused on the appearance in wearing leather. He didn't want the whips and chains, nor the bondage or pain; instead he wanted the feel of the leather against his skin, its smoothness and softness caressing his body. He knew that just the touch of leather on his body could turn him on.

He wandered down a flight of stairs and landed up in a dungeon-like shop. He roamed around the shop admiring all the different leather outfits, jockstraps, waistcoats, caps and jeans, touching them to get the cool feel of the leather. Everywhere in the shop was dark with a few spot lights illuminating certain areas, and it had a sense of mystery about it; it was all black and silver – black of the leather and silver from the chrome objects.

A tall guy of approximately six foot six, in leather jeans and wearing a harness, came up to him and asked if he might help. He had broad shoulders, with a tattoo on his left bicep, and a trim waist. Mike looked at him and almost shot a load in his jeans. The guy was hot, but Mike was at a loss for words. Eventually he was able to speak.

"Hi. I'm looking for something leather to wear," Mike stammered, rather stupidly, instead of asking if Clint's friend worked there.

The salesman, with his shaved head, smiled at Mike, knowing that he was new to the leather scene from his embarrassment.

"Is this your first time of trying leather?" he asked, showing a sense of pity for this idiot who was confused by all the garments on display.

Mike nodded absent-mindedly, like a young child, except he was twenty-eight.

"I've always had a liking for leather but I don't know what to buy."

"Are you planning to go to the leather bars?"

Mike hadn't thought of things like that and so was once again dumbstruck.

"I think you must also decide what image you want to portray. How about us getting you a decent pair of leather jeans, because that is the basic item you need?"

"OK," Mike replied. "I'm a size 32."

"Right, come this way and let's see what we can find for you."

He led Mike to a section towards the back of the shop where there were rows and rows of leather jeans, and on seeing them, Mike's mind became more confused; but he needn't have worried, because the guy pulled three pairs off the rack and handed them to Mike.

"Here. These are all 32's, but in different designs. Why don't you go into the change room and try them on."

Mike followed the direction of the salesman's hand and took them into the change room, which was relatively small and had a full-length mirror against one of the walls. He stripped down to his briefs and slid on the first pair.

They fitted beautifully and when he turned around and looked in the mirror, he could see how they accentuated his firm ass; he liked these. He removed those and tried on the second and third pairs, and as he was trying on the last pair, the salesman came into the change room.

"How's it going?" he asked. "These fit kinda tight," he said patting Mike's ass.

Mike looked in the mirror and knew that before the guy had tapped his ass with his hand, he had already started to get a hard-on which was evident in the mirror.

"I can see you like these," the salesman said, smiling at Mike in the mirror, and focusing his eyes on Mike's bulging crotch. "Now let's get you some attachments we can add to this outfit."

He disappeared for a moment and returned with a handful of other pieces of clothing and accoutrement, such as a studded collar, belts, waistcoat, leather jockstrap, some chaps and a harness.

"Try these on and let's see what you look like."

The first item that Mike picked up was the harness and didn't know how to put it on, so the salesman, who had remained in the change room, helped.

"What's this?" asked Mike, looking at the leather attachment which had a large metal ring attached to it.

The salesman smiled and said, "It's a cock ring attached to the harness."

All Mike could say was "Oh!" rather stupidly.

"Come on, take off these jeans and let's get you dressed properly."

Mike was embarrassed to take off the jeans considering that he knew that he had such a hard-on underneath, but with constant jibbing from the salesman, he did as he was told. The jeans came off.

"And the briefs," the salesman instructed.

Down they came and there stood Mike with his massive erection for the salesman to see.

"You're quite a big boy, aren't you?" commented the salesman, smiling at what he saw.

Mike blushed and tried to cover up his erection, but without success.

"Slip your cock and balls through the ring," said the salesman, trying to show Mike how, "if you can get that big thing through there."

They battled, because of Mike's erection, but between the two of them they eventually managed to get everything through, much to Mike's delight, especially having had the giant of a man, feeling his hard-on and balls.

"How's that feel?"

"Tight and makes me even more horny," Mike replied, without thinking and watching his cock throbbing in the mirror.

"That's what it's there for; now slip on these jocks," he said, handing Mike the leather jockstrap.

Mike slipped them on and tried desperately to fit his cock into them, but it remained peeping over the top of the waistband.

"Never mind about that, but I see you're leaking a bit," the salesman said and wiped a finger across the tip of Mike's cock, scooped up some of his pre-cum and licked it off his finger. "Hm! Tasty! Now let's try the chaps."

Again Mike did as he was told and he soon realized that his whole appearance was beginning to change. The salesman stood back to admire his model, then picked up the collar.

"Let's put this on and see how you look."

The collar was placed around Mike's neck and the studs shone in the change room light.

"I think that just about makes you complete. What do you think?"

Mike looked at himself in the mirror, turning in all directions to see front and back views.

"I like this, but I suppose I'll just have to get used to being a walking hard-on," he answered.

The salesman laughed. "Well there's nothing wrong with that, and with what I've seen between your legs, you've got nothing to worry about, the guys will be falling all over you."

"Thanks for the compliment, but you don't think I'm overdoing it with all the leather?"

"Not at all. That's what you want isn't it? If you feel that there's too much showing by wearing the chaps, you can always wear your leather jeans instead of the chaps, or you could also wear the chaps over an ordinary pair of jeans, if you wanted to."

Mike nodded in agreement and so it was that he bought his first complete leather outfit.

"By the way, I'm Mike," he said extending a hand to shake the salesman's.

"Hi, I'm Mitch."

"Are you Clint's friend?"

"Clint the American Airlines' flight steward?"

"Yes, the same guy. I met him last night on my flight from New York."

"Sure, Clint and I are good buddies. He usually touches base with me whenever he's in London."

"Well, in that case, I'm sure he'll be in touch. But tell me Mitch, there's just one other thing I need to know – where am I going to wear these?"

He roared with laughter and said, "At the leather bars and clubs, of course."

"But I've never been to one before and I certainly don't know where any are here in London."

"Listen Mike, there's a Mr. Leather competition being held at the Hoist on Saturday night; why don't you meet me there and I'll show you around? And wear the new clothes!"

Mike liked the idea and Mitch's friendly nature.

"Thanks Mitch, I'd really appreciate that, but you'll have to give me directions. At least if you're there, I won't feel so out wearing my new leathers."

"Trust me, you won't."

Mike eventually managed to lose his erection, paid for his goods and headed back home to his hotel. He was happy with his purchases and more than happy that he had made friends with Mitch. At least he now had a contact in London.

Mike phoned the States to tell his family that he'd arrived safely in London, but never said a word about his latest leather acquisition. Barry wanted to know whether he'd been out yet, to which Mike informed him that there was a vast time difference between the two countries, so he hadn't had time yet, but he didn't inform his inquisitive nephew that he would be visiting a leather club before the week was out.

Before the weekend arrived, Mike had visited most of the bars in Soho's Old Compton Street and was most impressed by the majority of the men he saw there. Naturally, he was also a popular sight to many men, who tried to get him to go with them, but Mike was in no hurry to bed the first person he saw.

Saturday eventually arrived and a sense of excitement ran through Mike, knowing that he was going on an adventure that night. He wasn't sure exactly why he was doing this, but an innate sense told him that he had always wanted to do it. At seven that evening he showered and began to get dressed. Fortunately he managed to put on the harness and the cock ring before he gave himself a hard-on, but no sooner had he got it on, than his cock began a life of its own, rising and getting bigger each minute. His jocks and leather jeans were slipped on and he admired himself in the mirror. Even with only those items on Mike decided that he looked sexy – maybe he'd leave the dog collar behind tonight. He was now ready for action. Suddenly a thought flashed into Mike's mind – how was he going to get to the club dressed the way that he was? If he went on the underground, people would stare, and he was sure that he'd feel embarrassed, so instead he chose to call a cab and get there by those means.

Mitch and Mike had agreed to meet outside the Hoist bar and club, but when Mike arrived he realized what Mitch had meant – everyone was hanging around and everyone was in leather, so he didn't feel out of place. There were old guys and young guys, well-built ones and ordinary guys, some with dog collars and chains attached, being dragged by their partners and others in jockstraps and chaps, which he decided was incredibly sexy, but which he'd been afraid to wear on that night.

"Mike! Over here!" he heard Mitch call.

Mike wandered over to where the tall, well-built Mitch was standing and admired his outfit. He was simply dressed in a pair of tight-fitting leather jeans and had on his bald head a black leather cap. His muscular chest was bare except for the beautiful tattoo which stretched across from his left bicep over his left shoulder onto his chest and over his left nipple. The design was almost floral with swirls and what looked like ornate leaves. Mike's attention went to Mitch's chest and the intriguing design, then he noticed his ripe nipples – they were firm, large and extended a good half inch from his proud pecs. Although he was simply dressed, his height and majesty made him stand out in the crowd. A few of Mitch's friends came up and spoke to him and as soon as the doors opened, everyone flooded into the bar.

It was a fairly dark place with a heavy metallic décor theme. The stairs were metal, the bar counter metal and the bar stools were also metal but had black leather padding on them, and the limited lighting that there was, had metal light shades. Music was blaring over hidden speakers and drinks were beginning to flow.

"Before things hot up here, let me show you around," said Mitch taking Mike's arm and leading him on a tour of the premises.

There were three floors to the bar; street level, where the main bar was; a basement area which had toilets and a couple of spaces where there were slings and St Andrews crosses, and a small upper area, which had a maze with some glory holes and dark corners. It wasn't necessary for Mitch to explain each of these areas in detail as Mike was well aware of the various options available, but he found it interesting how Mitch made each area sound sexy and elaborated on how they might be used. Mike took it to mean that he had much experience of using these various areas.

Mitch and Mike made their way back to the ground floor to get some beers and to survey the scene. Mike stood looking at the guys who were arriving at the bar and saw how they all looked like clones: leather everywhere, but the strong, overwhelming aroma of leather was a turn on for him. He could feel himself getting worked up by the intense masculinity that was evident in the bar. Everywhere he looked he could see black and silver and men preening themselves. Naked flesh was in abundance. The number of men who were semi-naked made it all the more exciting for him. Their muscles had been pumped and some had even gone to the trouble of smearing a thin layer of oil over their naked flesh, so that it glistened in the light and emphasized their muscles more. Maybe this was why Mitch had arrived without anything covering his chest, except for a slightly oily sheen.

"Are you taking part in the competition, Mitch?"

He nodded and smiled at Mike. "But I can see some stiff competition here tonight," he added.

Mike looked around and noticed about thirty other guys who might be taking part, but wasn't sure.

"What criteria do they look for in these competitions?" Mike asked, innocently.

"Oh, there're a few factors to be considered: it's not just the leather that you're wearing but how you look in the leather."

"Is that all?"

Mitch laughed.

"No, there is something else that's taken into consideration in competitions held here."

"What's that?"

"You might find that part interesting," he replied, winking at Mike.

"So what is it?"

"Wait. You'll see later."

Music was blaring over the speakers and the noise level both from people shouting to one another and the music, created a frenetic scene. Drinks flowed profusely and Mike was introduced to quite a few of Mitch's friends, some of whom showed a definite interest in Mike.

Suddenly, at 11.00pm, the music stopped and a voice was heard over a microphone telling all the potential contestants to meet below the small stage which had been erected near the dance floor. Mitch and the others began moving there where their names were taken and each had a number written on their arm. Mitch had a seven in red lipstick written on his right bicep. The contestants then lined up in numerical order and waited for the competition to begin. As each number was called, so that contestant mounted the stage, posed for the crowd and then walked up to a bar stool that had been placed on the stage, where the 'other' judging took place. Mike became fascinated by the 'other' judging.

The first six guys made their way across the stage, some looking very inviting, Mike thought, and then it was Mitch's turn.

Mitch mounted the stage and immediately struck a pose with the spotlight glistening on his buffed body. As he stood there in the light, it was clear that he had no jockstrap or briefs under his tight jeans, as the complete outline of his huge cock lay down the left leg of his jeans, revealed to the world. He posed, just as a bodybuilder might, flexing his muscles and smiling to all, then he strutted over to the bar stool. There was a hushed silence as he slowly began to unzip his leather jeans. Mitch pulled the front of his jeans open and inserted his hand. He pulled out his massive cock with its long shaft and bulging cut head and laid it on the leather barstool seat. The audience gasped. The judge took his ruler, laid it alongside the long muscle and measured.

"Eleven inches!" exclaimed the judge.

Immediately there were cheers, shouts, whistles and applause. A broad smile covered Mike's face. He couldn't believe that Mitch was SOOO big, but he was pretty proud of him. Now he understood why Clint had said that Mitch was 'big'. Not only was the man large in height, but he was huge, not big, between his legs. Mitch stood there after the measuring had been completed allowing his long, flaccid cock to be admired by the crowd, then he slowly and seductively began to tuck it back into his leather jeans and adjust its lie, then he zipped up again and left the stage. Everyone was crowding around Mitch as he fought his way to where Mike was standing.

"Wow, you were great!" Mike said, excitedly when Mitch reached him. "But the measuring was a total surprise to me."

"I told you this competition was different from other leather ones."

People were trying to speak to Mitch and guys were touching him and patting him on his shoulder as though he had already won the competition. Mike didn't feel at all jealous with all the attention Mitch was getting, but Mike could see that most of the guys coming up to him had one thing in mind; they wanted that cock! But then having seen it, so did he want it!

The competition continued with some really hunky looking guys coming on stage, who looked stunning in their various leather outfits, but when it came to cock size, Mitch won hands down. After the last competitor had done his thing on the stage, the judges grouped together to decide on their results. The MC picked up the microphone to announce the results.

"Gentlemen, we have seen some really hot, hot men here tonight and I can see from the way some of you have been drooling, you'd like to whip any of them into bed with you, but before you can do that, we need to announce our results. Tonight, we have a tie for third place."

He gave the numbers of the contestants and both guys went up on stage to receive their prizes, which included leather goods, money and a sash. The second placed contestant was called and a young guy of about twenty-four with a really buffed chest encased in a harness, a studded collar around his neck and tight leather jeans made his way up on stage. Mike remembered that his cock was a good length when he'd laid it on the bar stool and he remembered thinking he might be nice to spend a night with.

"In first place and Mr. Leather 2008, number seven," shouted the MC.

Mitch strode proudly up to the stage while everyone cheered once more. He took the stage with an air of confidence and power and when he had his sash placed across his bare chest, as an encore, he slowly began to unzip his jeans. The crowd went wild with excitement at the prospect of seeing that massive weapon of his again, but at the last minute, he zipped up again – he sure knew how to tease!

It took him longer to reach Mike as more guys tried to hog his attention and get to touch him. Eventually when he reached Mike, Mike looked up at this giant of a man and asked, "May I give the winner a kiss?"

Mitch didn't say a word, but grabbed Mike, hugged him to his muscular chest and their mouths met. Mike could feel the long shaft pressing against him and as they continued to kiss, there was a distinct changing in the hardness of their cocks. Mike could feel Mitch's erection growing and jabbing into him, but Mike wasn't about to let the other guys get their hands on him.

Mitch broke free and whispered in Mike's ear, "Let's go downstairs where it might be a bit quieter." He took Mike's hand and led him through the throngs to the stairs leading downstairs. Naturally there were some guys who chose to follow them, in the hopes that Mitch might take note of them.

When they reached the cavernous basement, Mitch took Mike to one of the areas where there was a sling.

"Do you know what would be the most valued prize for me tonight?" he asked, smiling at Mike.

Mike pretended he didn't know what Mitch was getting at.

"I'd like to get into your tight little ass," he continued.

It was Mike's turn to smile. Without hesitation, he stripped off his jeans and jockstrap and willingly climbed into the sling. Mitch gently raised Mike's legs and rested them on the chains hanging from the ceiling and then began to work on his body. Mitch's mouth explored every inch of Mike's body, bringing with it waves of ecstasy as his tongue touched different erogenous zones. Mitch's tongue explored the length of Mike's firm legs, licking and kissing them as he headed down towards Mike's crotch. By the time Mitch's mouth and tongue reached Mike's balls, Mike's cock was dribbling pre-cum which Mitch casually licked off and continued his journey over Mike's naked body. His tongue found its way to Mike's waiting ass, which he spread wider and attacked Mike's pucker, lubricating it until his spit dribbled down Mike's ass cheeks.

Mitch stood up and unzipped his leathers, all the while looking into Mike's eyes. He withdrew his extended, hard cock, holding his shaft firmly, and aimed it at Mike's entrance. Mike tensed as he anticipated the invasion, but he longed for the feeling of Mitch's long, thick shaft sinking into his depths. Slowly Mitch forced his way into Mike's warm chute. Mike could feel the broad cock-head spreading his opening and the feel of excitement hit him. Mike desperately wanted Mitch inside of him so he pushed to meet Mitch's thrust. Suddenly Mitch's shaft sank deeply into Mike's opening. Both of them sighed loudly as Mitch sank deeper and deeper into Mike until his hips came to rest against Mike's ass cheeks. They both smiled at each other as Mike allowed himself the pleasure of feeling Mitch's massive cock slowly expand his ass chute.

Holding onto the chains of the sling, Mitch began to slip in and out of Mike's throbbing ass. He would allow his cock to exit completely, leaving Mike with an empty feeling, and then he'd ram it back in, driving his young friend crazy with desire. The sling was swinging and the chains were rattling with each thrust so it wasn't necessary for Mike to exert pressure to meet his thrusts. As he plowed into Mike's tight ass, they both noticed a few other leather guys who had followed them, standing watching Mitch get off, stroking themselves, but none venturing to join in. Mike thought they knew that he was Mitch's prize and not for anyone else's consumption, as it were.

Mitch leaned forward as he plowed into Mike's ass and sucked on his young conquest's throbbing cock. As he did this, Mike took hold of Mitch's ripe nipples that were ready for chewing on, and pinched them between his fingers. He knew Mitch liked the feeling because as he pinched them tightly, so Mitch thrust harder into Mike's ass and groaned enthusiastically.

Their combined breathing was becoming more intense and heavier and they knew that they were both nearing the moment they'd been waiting for.

"Mitch, you're getting me close. I'm gonna shoot," Mike gasped as Mitch plunged into him once more.

"So am I," he grunted, holding onto Mike's hips for support and speeding up his thrusts.

Mike felt the large cock-head swell inside him and as he let fly with his first load of a number of shots of warm cum, so he felt the spasms as Mitch shot his load. Mitch's cock throbbed as he continued plowing into Mike's ass as he shot his load, and with each shot Mike felt the throb of Mitch's long cock, nudging his prostate as it did so. Again Mitch leaned forward, but this time in search of Mike's mouth and their tongues met. As their climax began to subside and with their mouths still clamped firmly together, Mike could feel how Mitch's chest rubbed over Mike's wet stomach and chest, massaging his warm cum over his own body. After a good few minutes, Mitch slid his semi-hard cock from Mike's ass, but remained clasped to him, kissing. Mike could feel the long shaft rest against his own waning cock and together they throbbed.

"Welcome to the leather world, Mike. You'll do well in this world, especially with me around to tame that fine ass of yours. I hope this is not going to be the last time I get access to that tight hole."

Mike liked his compliment and replied, "so long as you take care of me and teach me everything about the leather world, I'll be your slave."

Mitch smiled, but added, "I don't need a slave. I want a buddy."

Mitch helped Mike from the sling and those who had been watching with envy, suddenly disappeared, but probably hoped for another day when perhaps Mike wouldn't be there and Mitch might get hold of one of their asses to fuck with that massive cock of his.

After Mike had experienced his real initiation into the leather world, he seemed to float through air as he made his way back to his hotel. If this was how his holiday was going to be, then he was in his seventh heaven.

The following day, he phoned Mitch to thank him for the previous evening and they decided to meet for lunch. At lunch, Mitch expressed his desire to meet Mike again that evening, but this time he was taking Mike to visit a friend.

At the agreed upon time, Mitch arrived at Mike's hotel in a cab and they set off to meet Mitch's friend.

"Who are we going to see?" asked Mike as the cab traveled through the busy London streets.

"Wait. You'll see when we get there," replied Mitch.

They drove for what seemed like at least half an hour before the cab pulled up in front of a hotel.

"What are we doing here?" asked Mike.

"I told you we were coming to see a friend of mine."

They made their way into the foyer of the hotel where Mitch asked at the reception desk if a certain person was in. The receptionist checked to see if the bedroom key had been handed in suggesting that the person had gone out.

"He should be up in his room," announced the receptionist.

Mike and Mitch got into the elevator and made their way up to the fifth floor where they looked for room 517. On finding it they knocked and waited. The door eventually opened and there stood Clint.

"Clint!" exclaimed Mike, on seeing him.

"Come in you guys."

Clint hugged Mitch; or rather the muscular man grabbed Clint in a bear hug, crushing him to his chest.

"Hi bud. It's so good to see you again," said Mitch, carrying Clint back into the room and diving with him onto the double bed, their bodies and lips glued to each other's.

Mike followed them into the room and closed the door behind him, smiling at their antics. He stood at the base of the bed while Mitch rapidly began stripping Clint's clothes from him. Obviously the two friends hadn't seen each other for quite some time and they were in a hurry to make up for lost time. Mike began to become a little embarrassed by being the voyeur to their love-making and wasn't sure what to do, so he quietly reopened the bedroom door, slipped out and closed the door gently behind him, and then made his way down to the hotel lounge to sit and wait for Mitch.

Over an hour later, both Clint and Mitch walked into the lounge of the hotel.

"Where did you get to?" boomed Mitch.

"I thought you might want to be alone together," answered Mike, "seeing that you haven't seen each other for a long time."

"Bullshit! We were hoping that you'd join in with us," continued Mitch.

Mike looked at Clint as if to apologize, but Clint simply added to his chastisement.

"Aren't you into threesomes?" asked Clint. "I was hoping we could have had a good session together."

Mike felt really bad having left them, but he didn't know what their plans were.

"Next time tell me what you're planning," was all that Mike could offer, although deep down he felt unhappy that he hadn't been party to their plan, as he'd found Clint an engaging young man when he'd met him on the plane to London and Mitch was, to say the least, big and enjoyable!

The three sat together in the lounge of the hotel and ordered drinks and Mitch was keen to tell Clint about his victory in the Mr. Leather competition and also shared his excitement with Clint of what happened in the basement of the bar between him and Mike.

"This guy's hung like a horse," said Mitch, referring to Mike. "You'd like that cock of his in you little ass," he added.

Mike laughed at Mitch's comment.

"You're the horse-hung dude, and I'm sure that both Clint and I should know."

Clint was just as excited for Mitch, but also a little envious at not being able to share the moment with Mike.

"How long are you staying in London, Mike?" asked Clint.

"I'm only here for another four days and then I'm off to Amsterdam."

"Ooh!" cooed Clint. "That should be fun. Do you know anyone there?"

"I don't know anyone over here or in Europe," replied Mike, "but it's not going to stop me from enjoying myself."

"You have to visit some of the bars in Warmoesstraat while you're in Amsterdam," said Mitch, with a twinkle in his eye.

"Why, what happens there?"

"You'll have every opportunity to wear your new leather outfits there, but be careful, that's all I'll say," responded Mitch, grinning from ear to ear.

"That looks like a wicked grin; what's going through your head, Mitch?" asked Mike.

"Let's just say you should have a great time there, with your good looks and great body."

The drinks flowed until well into the night and eventually at midnight, Mitch said that he needed to get home as he had to get up the following morning for work.

"You two are lucky because you're both on holiday, so you can sleep in."

Mike hadn't given sleeping in any thought, but once Mitch made this observation, Mike's face lit up and so did Clint's.

"Mike, I must be going. Do you want to share a cab with me back to your hotel?" asked Mitch.

Mike glanced across to Clint who shrugged his shoulders as if to say, 'your decision'.

"Thanks Mitch, but if it's OK with Clint, I think I'll stay a little longer and maybe have another drink with him."

"That's fine by me," answered Clint, happily.

"Well in that case, let me head home. I'll be in touch with you guys," said Mitch as he headed outside to call a cab.

Once he had gone, Clint looked at Mike and smiled.

"Would you like to come up to the room for another drink?"

Mike returned the smile and nodded.

The two men caught the elevator up to the fifth floor, entered Clint's room and immediately began to tear each others clothes off.

As the sun rose on a bright London morning, Mike and Clint lay cuddled together in the hotel bed, arms around each other, having spent a passionate night together.

For the remainder of Mike's stay in London, he spent much of his time with Mitch, visiting bars and enjoying each other's company, especially after Clint had to go back to work on a flight back to the States.

AMSTERDAM

Although Mike wasn't an avid reader, except for his forays into Oscar Wilde's little sayings which he enjoyed, he had read a couple of books on Holland, finding out about the history, cities to visit and things to do, so that on arrival, he wouldn't be at a loss as to what to do.

The first country, after England, he had chosen on his trip was The Netherlands, or as most people called it, Holland, not only to enjoy the sights and sounds of Amsterdam, but he also wanted to taste the decadent night life of this illustrious city.

Mike packed his suitcase, boarded the KLM plane from London and flew to Amsterdam. When he arrived at Schipol Airport in the early morning, he made his way to the railway station at the airport and caught a train into the center of the city. Once he left the Central Station, he made his way to the information offices across the road from the station and asked a charming young lady about accommodation. He felt surprised that she didn't seem concerned by the fact that he had asked for gay accommodation, and then he remembered reading an article in which it stated how liberal and open-minded the Dutch were. She phoned up a few places and then hit the jackpot. A single room was available in a small hotel near the Leidseplein, so, after having been given directions by the charming young lady, he caught one of the trams that headed in that direction and eventually got off when it reached Prinsengracht, which was a canal. He crossed the canal and soon found the hotel and made his way up a flight of stairs to the reception area to book in.

It was a quaint little hotel which offered a limited breakfast, which suited Mike. As is the case with many Dutch buildings, the buildings are tall and narrow so, after having booked in at the reception area, he had to climb a very steep, narrow staircase to reach his bedroom. It made him smile because it made him think of the buildings that he had constructed and how fortunate people back home were, not having such steep stairways in their homes. When he reached his room, he was actually surprised at how spacious it was even though he had thought they might be cramped. After he had unpacked his suitcase, he went back to the reception area and spoke to the receptionist, asking where things were. The receptionist, who can only be described as a pretty, young man of about twenty, handed him a map of all the main gay areas in Amsterdam.

"I think this might help you," he said, handing Mike the map, "but if you need any extra information, please don't hesitate to ask."

"Thanks," said Mike, smiling at the pretty, young man and taking the map and sitting in one of the armchairs in the reception area. He studied the map for some time to get his bearings, then he shouted across the reception area, which was empty, to the young man, "By the way, what's your name?"

"Hans," came the reply.

"Well, tell me, Hans, what do people usually do here at night? I mean do they go out early or do they go to bars first and then go on to clubs?"

"I would say that most go to bars first and then they go out clubbing later, but nothing really happens before 10 p.m. and in some cases, things only start after midnight."

"And what about saunas?" enquired Mike.

"Do you like saunas?" asked Hans.

"Oh yes," came the reply.

"Well we have one here in the hotel for the guests, but otherwise, there are the Thermos Day and Night saunas."

"Are they close by or do I need to get a cab?"

"Oh, both are very close, but for most things in Amsterdam, you don't need to get a cab."

"What time do they open?" asked Mike.

"The Day sauna usually opens at mid-day, while the Night one opens at about 11p.m and stays open until 8 a.m."

"Gee, thanks Hans that sounds great. Well, I think I'll go for a little walk around the city and find my bearings," said Mike, folding up his map and placing it in his shirt pocket.

Mike headed off towards the center of the city, admiring the beautiful old buildings as he did so, until he eventually reached the Dam Square. Using his map as a guide, he headed down a small street called Warmoesstraat. He remembered that this was the street that Mitch had mentioned to him. On his map, this was marked off as a gay area full of clubs and bars. As it was still early in the day, most of these clubs and bars were closed, so Mike was a little disillusioned by the drabness of the area. However, he passed a sex shop and looked into the window. There was an array of sex toys and videos, much like he'd seen in a few shops in L.A and places like that. He decided to take a closer look so he ventured into the shop and started looking around.

"Are you looking for anything special?" asked the shop assistant, a stocky man with a little moustache.

"No. I'm just looking around," replied Mike.

He continued looking at the various toys and picked up some of the video boxes to see the photos on them.

"Are you interested in videos?" asked the assistant.

"I do like them," said Mike.

"Do you want to go into the cinema and watch a video?"

"Do you have a cinema here?" asked Mike.

"Just through that door," answered the surly assistant.

Mike was told how much it cost to go into the cinema, paid his Euros and entered into the dark world of the cinema. It took some time for his eyes to adjust to the darkness, but soon he could see about a dozen people sitting watching a gay sex movie. He found himself a seat and relaxed to watch the film. As he sat there watching, he noticed that some of the audience were getting out of their seats and walking towards the screen and then going around the back of it. Some would stay out of sight for quite some time, while others seemed to return to their seats fairly quickly. He thought that perhaps the toilets were behind the screen, but curiosity got the better of Mike, so he rose from his seat and went the way that the others had gone.

When he got to behind the screen, it was very dark so he didn't move until his eyes once again got used to the darkness. He could hear sounds, but wasn't sure whether it was the heavy breathing and groans coming from the actors on the screen, or whether it was coming from people behind the screen. He slowly ventured towards where the sounds were coming from. He felt along a wall until there was an opening, obviously a doorway. He felt his way through the doorway and entered a large room. He could now hear the heavy breathing more clearly. There were other people in this room. Again, feeling his way along the walls, he ventured around the room. Occasionally, he bumped into somebody and there would be a quick feel, but he wasn't able to see the person. He neared to the heavy breathing. In fact it was right next to him. He put out both his hands to feel his way. His left hand touched somebody so he turned towards the person, but in doing so, he bumped into someone else. As he did this, a hand shot to his crotch and grabbed his balls and cock, almost as quickly as a piranha fish might grab a meal. He felt a hand unzip his jeans and slide into them. He then felt someone behind him, rubbing their hands over his ass. He presumed that the hands that were working on his cock didn't belong to the hands that were rubbing his ass. He just stood there enjoying his first taste of Amsterdam. Someone undid his jeans and he felt them fall to the ground. Soon after, he felt a warm mouth encircle his quickly rising dick. He pushed forward, forcing his cock down the person's throat. He could hear the slurping noise that the guy was making as he worked on Mike's dick. There were quite a few people in this room, because he soon felt a number of other people close in on him. Soon, hands were running all over his body. He could feel fingers trying to gain entry into his ass, and squeezing his nipples. Soon he heard somebody gasping and breathing heavily and felt warmness hit his right leg and felt someone's cum run down his thigh. People were groaning all around him as they were nearing their climaxes, and when Mike heard this, added to the fact that his cock was throbbing and wanting to shoot its load, he couldn't hold on any more and shouted above the groans, "I'm coming!"

The action around him speeded up. Mike felt the first shots exit from his cock and let out a groan as it did so. Others were also shooting their loads, and cum was flying in all directions. When Mike had exhausted everything in him, he pulled up his jeans and felt his way towards the light. He returned to his seat for a while to see if any of the others from the room might appear, so he could see what they looked like, but no one appeared, so he decided to leave the cinema. As he exited the cinema and went back into the main shop area, he saw the assistant and said, "Is there a toilet here?"

The assistant looked down at Mike's cum covered jeans, smiled and said, "Through that door."

Mike went into the toilet and tried to clean himself and his jeans. The stains on his jeans were difficult to get rid of, so he washed as much off as he could and pulled his shirt out of his jeans to try and cover the stains.

When Mike left the shop, he felt self-conscious and wondered if the stains were showing, so he kept pulling down his shirt in the front. He continued wandering around the streets until he found that he had unintentionally made his way back to the area in which the hotel was situated.

When he entered the foyer of the hotel, Hans was still behind the desk.

"Have you had a good day?" smiled Hans.

"Yes thanks," said Mike.

"What did you do?" enquired Hans.

"I just wandered around the city to get my bearings."

"Did you see anything that you liked?" asked Hans.

Mike wasn't sure whether he should say anything about the cinema to Hans, but after a moment's hesitation, he responded.

"I found a cinema," said Mike blushing as he said this.

"I'm sure that you had a good time there," laughed Hans.

Mike then laughed as well, feeling more at ease with Hans. "Actually, that's why I've got my shirt hanging out," said Mike.

"Oh, was somebody's aim not so good?"

"I suppose you could say that," replied Mike. "I think I'm going to go upstairs and clean up and have a rest before tonight."

At that, Mike ascended the steep staircase towards his bedroom, where he stripped off his jeans, cleaned them properly and lay down on his bed to have a short sleep.

Early that evening, after Mike had changed, he went downstairs ready to see the night-life that Amsterdam had to offer. Hans was still at the desk.

"Don't you ever go off duty?" asked Mike.

"Yes," came the reply. "In fact, I'm off duty in an hour's time," said Hans.

"Then you can go home and relax."

"Oh no, I stay here in the hotel, because there are times when we have an emergency and somebody has to be here to sort it out, so I stay on the premises."

Mike had found Hans to be an engaging young man, interesting to talk to, but although Hans was pretty, Mike didn't really find Hans to be his type of man. They stood chatting for quite a while in the reception area, until Mike decided to head off into the city once more.

"Well I think I'm going to go off to the Day sauna before going out to dinner," said Mike.

"I'm sure that you'll enjoy that," said Hans. "Maybe I'll see you when you come back."

"OK. Cheers," said Mike as he left the hotel.

He wandered aimlessly along the banks of the canals, following the direction on his map, until he knew that he was in the vicinity of the sauna that he sought.

He found his way to the sauna and went in and paid. The staff was extremely polite and he was told where his locker was situated and he climbed the stairs to the said area. As he made his was to his locker, he noticed how crowded the place seemed. Music was playing in the background, but it wasn't invasive at all. When he found his locker, he took off his shirt, pulled down his jeans and briefs and wrapped his towel around his waist. He locked his clothes away and made his way in the direction of the steam bath. On the way, he noticed how many men stared at him. He was aware that he had a finely tuned torso, but when he looked down he could see that his heavy cock, although not erect, was causing a protrusion in his towel. When he found the steam room, he entered to find about eight other men there already. He found a place to sit and did so. Silence rained; nobody was speaking.

He closed his eyes and relaxed while the steam and heat created sweat to run down his chest over his nipples and fall onto his dick. He undid his towel, put it across his lap and stretched his legs in front of him. His legs were muscular and well tanned. He opened his eyes and looked at his legs, admiring their development and wiping sweat from them and his chest. A guy of about thirty came and sat next to him, but said nothing. After a while, Mike felt the guy's leg touch his. He glanced across at the guy and through the steam, smiled because the guy looked pretty good looking. The guy obviously took this to be an invitation, because he put out a hand and rubbed it over Mike's leg.

"You've got great legs," said the guy.

"Thank you," replied Mike, and then looking again, he said, "so have you."

"In fact, you've got a great body. Do you work out?" asked his neighbour.

"No, but I'm in construction work, so I suppose I spend a lot of my time picking up heavy things. By the way, my name's Mike," he said, extending a hand to greet the guy next to him.

"Hi, I'm Franco."

"Are you on holiday here?" asked Mike.

"Yes, I've been here a couple of days. Are you also on holiday?"

"Yep, but I only arrived today," said Mike.

"And how do you like the place so far?"

"From what I've seen, I like it," said Mike.

All this time, Franco's hand had been rubbing up and down Mike's leg. Mike had enjoyed the touch of Franco's fingers as they slid over the sweaty, muscled thigh. Franco let his hand venture under Mike's towel, hoping that Mike wouldn't mind. When he felt Mike's dick he stopped, held it and said, "Oh my God, it feels so big."

Mike merely smiled at him. "I don't really think of it being big," said Mike, " but some people have said that it is."

Franco squeezed Mike's thickening dick. He lifted Mike's towel to reveal a ten-inch, cut, dick that rose from the constrictive towel. Mike lay back and admired his naked, sweat-drenched body while Franco's face was a picture of disbelief. Franco let his hand run gently over the length of Mike's cock.

"It just never seems to end," said Franco staring at this bargepole.

Mike held the base of his cock and said to Franco, "Do you want it?"

"Yes," gulped Franco. "But there's no way that you could fuck me with that, you'd split me," said Franco.

Franco slowly lowered his head over the tip of Mike's cock and let his wet tongue lick over it. He then licked down the length of Mike's cock until he reached his balls and took one and then the other into his mouth. He rolled them gently around his mouth and then let them pop out one at a time. He then worked his lips up Mike's length until he reached his cock-head and opening his mouth as wide as he could, began to swallow Mike's dick.

Mike lay there enjoying the pleasure while Franco slid his mouth down Mike's shaft until it touched the back of his throat. Franco thought he was going to gag, but managed to contain himself. He slowly slid up the length again and continued this until he felt that his throat muscles were getting used to the motion. Mike, in the meantime, held onto Franco's head forcing it to move up and down his cock.

Both men were sweating profusely from the action and the heat coming from the steam room. Mike ran his fingers over Franco's sweaty back and up through his hair. He grabbed onto Franco's hair and, forcing his head down, thrust his hips upwards to meet Franco's waiting throat. Franco pulled back and gasped. He looked at Mike, sweat pouring down his face.

"This cock tastes so good, but I wish I could take in its full length."

"You're doing fine," said Mike, wiping sweat from his eyes.

Both their bodies were saturated. Franco moved Mike's body so that Mike was now lying on his back on the tiled step that he had been sitting on. Franco positioned himself between Mike's legs and began to lick up each leg. When he reached Mike's crotch, he began sucking on Mike's balls again. Mike writhed in ecstasy as Franco worked over his balls and cock, licking and sucking. Franco then slid his chest over Mike's stomach and up to his chest. Their bodies glided together from the moisture in the room and when their mouths met, they clamped on to each other and their tongues fought a duel as though to the death. Franco rubbed his cock against Mike's and both thrust their hips into each other. Franco felt himself getting closer and let go of Mike's mouth.

"I'm going to come," he groaned.

"Come then," said Mike thrusting even harder into Franco's belly.

Franco gave a gasp and began to shoot over Mike's cock and stomach. He kept thrusting his cock onto Mike's stomach until he had emptied himself. As his body relaxed, he slid from Mike and lay on the step below. Mike lay there playing with his cock, sliding his hand up and down its length. Franco rose from where he was lying, kissed Mike's cock and said, "I'm going for a shower," and left the steam room.

Mike lay there feeling empty having not been able to be satisfied, but he continued to play with his cock. The door to the steam room opened and an elderly man came in. He looked at Mike and saw this huge dick and well-defined body. He couldn't contain himself, so he crossed hurriedly to where Mike was lying and took over the job that Franco had left of sliding a hand up and down its length. Mike opened his eyes and saw the old guy. At this stage, Mike didn't worry about age or looks; all he wanted to do was to get rid of the frustrated load that he was carrying in his balls. The old man worked feverishly on Mike's cock and Mike lay there, eyes now closed, thrusting up into the air. He felt himself getting nearer but never said anything. Finally, his balls moved closer to his belly, tightened and the first shots sprayed up into the air and fell onto his chest. As this happened, he let out a growl and fired off a quick succession of shots that landed on his stomach, as well as the old man's hand and over his own cock and balls. As soon as Mike had finished coming, the old man fled the steam room. Mike sat up and using some of the water that was lying on the tiles, from the steam, began to clean himself. When he was completed, he rose, wrapped his towel around himself, and with his still erect cock pushing the towel out in the front, he left the steam room.

Mike made his way to the showers where he cleaned himself properly and then went for something to drink, to put some liquids back into his body.

This was exactly the type of holiday Mike had wanted: one filled with unadulterated sexual energy and lust. Oh how nice it was to be alone on holiday, he thought. He could do as he pleased and didn't have to answer to anyone – except of course until his loving nephew would arrive, but he still had plenty of time before that would happen.

After resting for about half an hour, Mike decided that he had recovered sufficiently to start all over again. He was becoming a sex machine, something that he'd never considered back home in the States. Was this perhaps pent up frustration coming out, or was he just being an animal?

Mike decided to wander around the sauna complex, investigating various rooms. There were a number of rest cubicles where men lay, either alone, playing with themselves in the hope that someone would take the invitation and enter their cubicle, or with someone else. Mike then went past a swimming pool where athletic looking guys were casually swimming or diving. Near the swimming pool was the sauna. He entered and closed the door behind him. The intensity of the dry heat hit him. He sat on one of the benches and felt the heat penetrating the pores of his body. In one of the corners, two young guys were busy sucking each other off while a middle-aged man watched them intently and played with himself. Mike watched this action for a while and began to feel life coming back into his dick. He could feel it beginning to grow in size. He pushed down on his dick, trying to hide it, but that was no good. He watched the two guys and wondered whether he should join in, but then he thought against it and rose to leave. As he did so, the two young guys lifted their heads to see him. They saw his mighty erection under his towel. Mike left the sauna cabin and headed for the showers again. The two young guys immediately rose from their positions and watched through the glass window of the sauna door as Mike went into the shower area. They made eye contact with each other, opened the door and followed into the shower area.

The shower room had a number of small shower cubicles as well as an area where there were about three open showers. In the open shower area, were a number of guys busy playing with one another, each doing something to one of the others. The two young guys walked past some of the shower cubicles until they stopped in front of the one that Mike was standing under. Mike's head was thrown back as the refreshing water poured over his face and down his chest. His body looked majestic in the water and the steam from the shower. The two guys stared at this Greek god with a half erect ten-inch dick bouncing in the water and contemplated their action.

One of the two entered the shower cubicle, knelt in front of Mike, opened his mouth and took Mike's dick into it. Mike's head fell forward to see what was happening. He wiped the water from his eyes and looked down. The young guy kept his mouth over Mike's dick and looked up at Mike. Mike did nothing. He just let him carry on. When the other guy, who had been watching, saw this, he moved into the cubicle as well and got onto his knees. It was as though these two were worshipping their Greek god as they both tongued Mike. Their lips moved up and down its length and whenever their mouths reached the tip of Mike's dick, they kissed each other. They continued this action for some time and a few others came to watch what was happening in the shower cubicle. Another guy moved into the cubicle and started squeezing Mike's nipples. When he did this, Mike threw back his head in absolute pleasure. The guy then wrapped his lips around Mike's left nipple and began to chew on it gently.

"Harder," sighed Mike.

The man obeyed and chewed harder. In fact the more he bit on Mike's nipples, the more excited Mike became, and the more he thrust his dick into the waiting mouths of his two young worshippers. The nipple man's tongue ran over Mike's nipples, which were standing erect, and he made his way over to Mike's right nipple, where he repeated the whole process over again.

Mike pulled the nipple man closer to him and pulled his mouth up to meet his own. Their mouths parted and their tongues shot out to enter the other's mouth. Their attack of each other's mouth was almost violent, and as they attacked each other with kisses, one of the two young guys had taken Mike's dick into his mouth and was trying as hard as he could to get it down his throat. He pushed forward onto Mike's dick, relaxed his throat and went even further until the whole of Mike's dick was down the young man's throat. He held it there without moving, but the feeling was so great for Mike that he thrust forward. The young gasped and let go of Mike's dick. He coughed and regained his breath. While he was doing this, his friend took over. Meanwhile, Mike's wet fingers were trying to pry open the nipple man's ass cheeks so that he could slide a finger or two in there. The nipple man realized what Mike was trying to do, so he turned around to face the two guys on the floor. Mike's hand went straight to his own dick, which had been well and truly lubricated by the young mouths. He held it by the base to give it support, aimed for the nipple man's ass and pushed. As he entered him, the man let out a scream. Mike held his position.

"You push back when you're ready," Mike said.

He felt the man's ass pushing up against his dick, and all the while the man cried in pain, but refused to stop. Mike could feel that he was close to getting through the guy's sphincter. As he did, the guy let out a sigh of absolute pleasure. Mike held him tightly without moving while the guy got used to the huge size that was inside of him. Mike had an idea what this guy must be feeling because few guys had been able to take Mike's length and thickness, but it was also a great feeling for Mike as this guys ass tightened around his dick.

The two guys who were kneeling probably wished that Mike's huge dick was inside them, but it didn't stop them from enjoying seeing this great

32

fuck and being part of it. They resumed their sucking, but on the nipple man's cock.

Mike started gently to push forward and backward into the nipple man's ass and every time he went forward, the guy cried out in a combination of pain and ecstasy. Whenever the guy felt pain, he tensed and so tightened his ass muscles around Mike's dick, which in turn sent Mike into what felt like heaven and he would push even harder and deeper.

Mike pinched the guy's nipples and he thrust backward onto Mike's dick.

'Obviously', thought Mike, 'this guy gets off on this,' and squeezed harder. The more that Mike squeezed, the more frantic the guy pushed onto Mike's dick. The guy could feel Mike's huge bargepole rubbing against his prostate and he knew that he wouldn't be able to take much more.

"Aargh!" he groaned, making his movement frantic. "I'm coming!"

The guys on the floor fought to gain possession of his cock so that they could get his full taste. Suddenly he let out another cry and his body convulsed as he emptied his load into the waiting mouths below him. As he shot his first load, his sphincter tightened around Mike's dick. Mike wrapped his arms around the guy, pulling him closer to his own body, and pounded his cock into the hot, waiting ass. In fact, he pounded so hard, that his action sent one of the kneeling guys onto the floor. Once Mike had fired his supply into the guy, both he and the nipple man began to relax, and he slowly let his dick slide out and only then did he feel the man relax totally. The guy turned towards Mike, kissed him gently on the lips and said, "That's the greatest fuck I've ever had. I've never had anyone so big."

"Well, I'm glad you could take it," said Mike, kissing the guy again. "It's not often that I get to fuck anyone because people are frightened off by my size. Thanks again."

They helped to wash each other while the two young worshippers rose and left to look elsewhere for some action.

Mike showered and dressed and left the sauna, making his way to one of the many restaurants in Amsterdam. He found one and went in and had something to eat and a few drinks. He was feeling pretty exhausted from his first hectic day in Amsterdam, so he didn't stay long in the restaurant and left for the hotel.

When He arrived back at the hotel, Hans was sitting in the lounge.

"Back so early," he said.

"I've had quite an exhausting day so I thought I would have an early night."

"So, if you're exhausted, why don't you have a sauna before you go to bed and relax?"

Mike laughed, "I don't know if I could handle another sauna."

"Oh, so that's where you've been," said Hans. "Did you score there? Meet anyone interesting?"

Mike just smiled and nodded his head. He was beginning to like Hans, who tended to be a jovial and down to earth sort of guy. He had already noticed how he opened up to Hans more than he did to anyone back home.

"Well, I'm going to have a sauna before I go to bed," said Hans. "If you change your mind, you'll find the sauna on the first floor. If I don't see you, sleep well."

Hans made his way to the sauna, and Mike made his way to his room, which was also on the first floor. Mike went into the room, took off his clothes and fell onto the bed.

Hans took off his clothes and walked into the sauna. The heat was luxuriating and he stretched himself, naked along the bench in the sauna. He lay there on his back, wiping off the odd bit of sweat, which was accumulating on his chest. Mike lay naked on his bed, thinking about his day's activities. As his thoughts wandered, he visualized the cinema and its dark room, then he thought of the fun he had at the Day Sauna. He soon realized that these thoughts had brought about a hard-on. He pushed his cock downwards away from his stomach. When he let go, it shot back into its erect state like a catapult being fired. He got up from the bed, wrapped a towel around his waist, opened the bedroom door and walked down the passage to the sauna.

When Mike reached the sauna, he knew in his own mind why he had gone there, and it wasn't for the sauna. He opened the door. Hans turned his head to see who was coming in. When he saw Mike, he said, "I'm glad you made it," and closed his eyes again. Mike came into the sauna and sat on the bench at Hans's feet. He looked at Hans's young, hairless body and saw that his uncut cock was beginning to grow although nobody was touching it.

Mike said, "Hans, what are you thinking of?"

"You," came the reply.

"And what are you thinking?" asked Mike.

"You taking me."

"I don't know if I could do that, I'm exhausted."

"It's all right," said Hans, "I've already thought about that."

Mike leaned forward, opened his mouth and took Hans's cock into his deep throat.

Hans gave a whimper. "Oh Mike, that feels so good."

Mike released Hans's cock and said, "Was that also in your thoughts?"

"No, but it would be nice to have a bonus. Would you do it again?"

Mike obliged. He held Hans's cock and pulled on it, wrapping his mouth over it and letting his tongue go in under Hans's foreskin. Hans squirmed and thrust his hip upwards.

"Mmmmm! " groaned Mike, "this tastes good," and he pushed further down Hans's cock.

This continued for a while and then Hans raised his head and said to Mike, "Please come and lie on the bench."

Hans climbed off the bench to allow Mike to lie down. Once Mike was relaxed, Hans went to work on Mike's huge cock. He kissed, licked, sucked and caressed it as though it was the most precious thing in the world. Once Hans had made it wet, he lifted his head, climbed onto Mike's stomach and aimed Mike's cock at his ass.

"Are you going to sit on me?" asked Mike.

"Yes," said Hans. "I want you to relax, and I'm going to do the work."

He held Mike's dick at its base and guided it to his entrance. He felt the initial pain as its hugeness slowly penetrated him. He froze for a while to get used to its size, and then continued some more.

"Hans, if it's hurting, don't do it; we can just jerk each other off if you like."

"No, Mike. I want to give you pleasure as much as I want your pleasure," said Hans as he continued pushing.

Mike contemplated Hans's intention of giving him pleasure and a smile broke on his face. He'd had more pleasure in one day in Amsterdam than he'd had in a month back home.

Hans felt the head of Mike's dick pass his sphincter and he gave a sigh of relief. As the pain subsided, Hans sank onto Mike's full length and held his position there to get used to it.

Hans leaned forward to kiss Mike, and as he did so his ass rose up the length of Mike's dick. Mike immediately thrust his hips upwards because he didn't want his cock to slip out. Once their mouths were attached and busy, Hans started rising and falling onto Mike's dick. Mike enjoyed this position because he was tired and it allowed him to relax but still enjoy what was happening. It wasn't long before Hans realized that he was reaching his climax.

"Slow down, Mike, I'm getting close."

Mike laughed. "Me slow down, I'm not doing anything, you're the one who's doing the work."

Hans sat still on Mike's cock and could feel it throb inside of him. "I like it when you throb inside of me," said Hans.

"The only reason it's throbbing is because you're getting me worked up. I find what you're doing to me very sexy, and it turns me on."

"Do you really like this?" asked Hans.

"Hm, I like it when you do the fucking. I crave to see my dick sliding in and out of your ass, and the fact that you can take it all the way is an even bigger turn on," said Mike.

When Hans heard this, he started to speed up his action. He was very close now.

"Mike I'm coming, I'm going to shoot!"

"Go for it kid, ride my dick. Take it all the way! Harder!" And Mike started thrusting upwards.

Hans let out a cry and white fluid flew from his cock onto Mike's stomach. He kept shooting and riding Mike's cock, clenching his sphincter as he did so.

The tightness really turned Mike on and he gave a loud guttural cry.

"Fuck my cock! Oh yes! Oh baby, take this dick! Fuck it! Aaaargh!"

They were bouncing around on the sauna bench with Mike fucking Hans's ass as hard as he could. When they had emptied their load, Hans leaned forward and kissed Mike. Mike put his arms around Hans and they lay there for some time, kissing gently.

"Would you like to, or are you allowed to, spend the night with me?" asked Mike.

"Do you really mean that?"

"Are you allowed to?"

"Of course," said Hans.

They climbed off the bench, wrapped their towels around themselves and headed back to Mike's room where they slept like babies.

The following day, Hans woke to find Mike still holding him in his arms and Mike's erect cock pushed up against Hans's. Hans wasn't sure whether he should start something again, but chose to slip out of the bed instead.

Later that morning, when Mike came downstairs, Hans was at the reception desk.

"Hans, thanks for last night, I though it was very special," said Mike.

Hans just blushed. "You're quite a horny bugger, aren't you?"

"Why do you say that," asked Mike.

"Well you were hard again this morning."

"So why didn't you do something about it?"

Hans laughed and said, "I thought that maybe you'd had enough for a while. By the way, what are you planning on doing today?"

"I though I would go off to Rotterdam or one of those places."

"That would be nice. Well I hope you have a good day."

Hans left to start doing his day's work while Mike set off to do his tourist thing.

That evening, when Mike returned to the hotel, he found a note under his bedroom door, which read:

Dear Mike,

I'm going to the sauna around the corner from the hotel tonight – the one you went to yesterday. If you want to join me, I'll see you there.

Hans.

Mike gave it some thought, but decided he'd go for a drink before he went to the sauna. On the other hand, he might meet someone and not go to the sauna. He headed to a bar in Kerk Street, which was quite crowded. The atmosphere was a happy one and everyone seemed to know everyone else. He got chatting to a couple of guys who were from London and who were there on business, but he wasn't really interested in them sexually, so he decided to take Hans's suggestion and try the sauna again. Mike was also wondering how much of his chosen cities he was actually going to see. It seemed that he was spending more time in saunas and bars than doing any sightseeing, but when he tried to rationalize his actions, he decided that it was his intention to come to Europe and lose his virginity – although he had lost it years ago when he was still at school.

He arrived at the sauna, smiled at the guys at the reception, who recognized him from the previous day, paid, got undressed and headed for the steam room area, which he liked. He noticed that there were a lot more people in the evening than in the afternoons. He entered the steam room, and once his eyes had got used to the steam and the light, he saw what looked like an orgy taking place. There must have been about eight or nine guys getting into each other. He watched this for a while, his dick erect from the scene that he was watching, and looked to see if any of the guys attracted him. He saw a guy of about twenty-eight, with very short, cropped hair, muscular and good looking, who was being sucked off by a slightly older guy, while another guy was kissing him. Mike moved closer to the young guy and ran his hand over the smooth, wet butt of the guy. When the guy felt this, he stopped kissing and looked to see who it was. He looked at Mike and moved his mouth over to Mike so that he could continue kissing. He ran his hands over Mike's pecs and down his stomach until he reached Mike's erection. As he touched it, Mike's dick flinched and the guy grabbed it. When he realized the size of what he had in his hand, his eyes shot open wide and the kiss froze.

He removed his mouth and looked Mike in the face. "That's some dick you've got there, buddy."

Mike kept working his fingers in and out of the guy's ass, looked back at the guy and said, "that's some ass you've got there."

"Do you want to get out of here?" asked the guy.

"Where do you want to go to? Asked Mike.

"Let's go to one of the rest areas," he said.

"OK," said Mike, "lead on."

They left the steam room and made their way to find a vacant rest cubicle.

On the way there, Mike saw Hans.

"Hi, Hans," he shouted.

Hans turned to see him and moved towards Mike.

"Where are you going?" asked Hans, but as he said it, he realized that Mike was with another guy.

"We're going to a rest room," whispered Mike, and he and his new steam room friend went off.

Hans seemed a little disappointed, but accepted the fact that Mike had his own life to lead.

Mike and his friend found an empty rest room, went in and closed the door behind them.

In the room was a single bed mattress, which lay on the floor. Mike sat down on the mattress and the other guy followed. Mike introduced himself, and the other guy said his name was Jeff.

"What are you into?" asked Jeff.

"I like sucking, being sucked and fucking," said Mike. "I don't know whether I'm into other things like S & M, etc, because I've never tried it. What about you?"

"The same as you, but sometimes I don't mind a guy fucking me, but he's got to be special, otherwise nobody gets this butt."

"Well tell me, do I get that butt, or don't I?"

"With a dick that size, you sure get to taste this butt, but suck my dick first."

Mike felt for Jeff's cock and worked a little on his with his hand. He could feel it getting a little harder.

"Make my dick hard with your hot mouth," said Jeff.

Mike wrapped his mouth around Jeff's dick and proceeded to suck.

"Take it deeper and harder," commanded Jeff.

Again Mike obliged. Jeff pushed Mike's head down over his cock, forcing it deeper into Mike's throat.

"That's better, now make me hard like a rock."

Mike felt a strange sensation at being ordered around the way he was. Somehow it was turning him on. He was not used to this and he realized it might make him angry.

Jeff started face-fucking Mike. "Can't you do it harder?" he snapped.

Mike thrust his mouth deeply over Jeff's dick.

"Oh yes, that's better, you cock-sucker. You want this butt, you've got to work for it."

Mike released his grip and said, "How about sucking my dick for a change?"

Jeff just pushed Mike's head down and shouted, "keep sucking, you fucker!"

"Lie down on the mattress," said Mike, "it'll be easier."

Jeff lay down on his back on the mattress.

Mike positioned himself between Jeff's legs, wrapped his arms under Jeff's legs and lifted Jeff's butt off the mattress and into the air. As he did so, his hungry mouth clamped onto Jeff's throbbing dick.

"Oh yes, fucker! Go for it. Take it right down your throat!"

Mike was beginning to become angry with the way he was being instructed to do things, but the insults were making him feel sexier and hornier.

"Fuck my face, asshole," shouted Mike, and Jeff thrust high into the air, forcing his cock deeper into Mike's throat. Mike was enjoying this aggression. With his right hand, Mike slid it from under Jeff's butt and slapped him on the ass. The sting sent a quiver through Jeff and he pushed his cock upwards.

"Aargh, I'm going to fuck you," said Jeff, pumping harder.

Mike continued his action and every few moment, he would slap Jeff's ass again.

As Mike was kneeling between Jeff's legs, he lifted Jeff's ass higher into the air and rested it on his knees. He let go of Jeff's dick and let his tongue run over his balls, working his way down to Jeff's butt crack. All this was turning Jeff on. Although he liked to fuck other guys, Jeff knew what was coming his way and he admired a guy who had a bigger dick than his own.

Mike's tongue moved into the ass crack and Jeff writhed with pleasure.

"Push that hot tongue of yours in," said Jeff sternly.

Mike let his tongue merely touch the entrance.

"I said shove it in. Rim my ass, fucker!"

Mike refrained. He was going to make Jeff beg.

Jeff was now squirming his ass around in the air, and in between tongue licks, Mike would slap it.

Mike felt his own cock, which was fully erect, and felt the trickle of pre-cum oozing from his dick.

"Fuck me, fucker! Take my ass and split it open with you dick. I want you to fuck me."

"When I'm ready," muttered Mike.

Just as he said this, the cubicle door opened slightly and Mike could see Hans standing in the doorway. Jeff didn't see anything because his back and head were to the door. Mike suddenly thought of something.

"Fuck me!" shouted Jeff.

"But I thought you said that you like fucking other guys?"

"I do," shouted Jeff again, "but I want you to fuck me. Go for my ass. Push it in!"

Although Mike continued to work on Jeff, he beckoned to Hans to come in.

"I'm going to give you a treat," said Mike, placing the head of his dick at the entrance to Jeff's ass.

"Oh yes," cried Jeff, "push it in."

"How would you like a fuck?" asked Mike.

"For fuck sake, fuck me, you're driving me crazy!"

"Close your eyes then and I'll give you the fuck of your life."

Jeff closed his eyes and Mike beckoned to Hans to sit on Jeff's cock, while Mike slipped his dick into Jeff. Hans quietly positioned himself above Jeff and slowly lowered himself onto Jeff's bouncing dick. As Hans touched Jeff's dick, so Mike pushed into Jeff.

Jeff let out a cry. "Oh Fuuuuck!" As this happened, he opened his eyes and saw someone riding his cock. As Mike thrust forward, so Jeff thrust up into Hans.

"I'll fuck you both," said Jeff.

"No, Jeff, we're going to fuck you. We're going to give you something to remember us by."

As Mike's huge cock pounded into Jeff, going in all the way so that

Mike's ball were slapping up against Jeff's, so Jeff rode Hans's ass. Hans was enjoying this, and having Hans do this to him, Mike knew that Jeff was going to enjoy his fuck as much as he was going to enjoy his.

Hans didn't take long to come and shot onto Jeff's chest.

Although he had come, Hans never released his grip on Jeff's cock until he felt Jeff's cock swelling in his ass.

"Fuck me harder, I'm going to come!" shouted Jeff, holding onto Hans's waist. Hans bounced up and down on Jeff's cock while Mike pounded into Jeff.

Jeff let fly his hot cum into Hans, "Oh yes! Oh yes! Fuck me! Fuuuuck!" cried Jeff.

Hans felt the warm sticky cum enter his ass and could feel some of it sliding down Jeff's dick.

Mike's climax was close and he pushed as though he wanted to get his balls into Jeff's ass. He held onto Hans for support and pushed Jeff's legs higher into the air, causing Hans to lie across Jeff's chest. Jeff and Hans's mouths met and their tongues fought for possession. Hans could feel that Jeff's cock was still very hard inside of him, so he carried on riding it as the two of them kissed.

"Fucker, you're getting it," shouted Mike as he pushed deeply into Jeff and held it there while the first shot emptied into Jeff's bowels. Once he had shot his first load, Mike rapidly pounded Jeff's ass. Hans could feel Jeff's cock throbbing inside his ass and he wanted this to carry on and not to stop.

When Mike had emptied everything he had into Jeff, he leant across Hans's back. Slowly he let his still throbbing dick slide from Jeff. As it did, Jeff sighed with relief, but Hans still stayed glued onto Jeff's cock. Mike rolled away from them and Hans sought Jeff's lips again. He found them and they passionately kissed each other. Hans continued to work on Jeff's cock, trying to keep it hard, and he was succeeding. He felt Jeff reciprocating every time he thrust down. Jeff would thrust upwards. Soon their actions became more active and Hans was once again bouncing on Jeff's dick. Mike just sat and watched this, playing with his own dick. After a while, Hans let out a cry again and shot onto Jeff's chest again. As his sphincter clamped around Jeff's dick and tightened, Jeff let fly his load and fucked that cute ass of Hans's. After Hans had come, he slipped off Jeff's dick, lay next to him and began to lick his cum off Jeff's chest.

"Now who got fucked?" asked Mike.

Jeff burst out laughing. "I suppose I got fucked, but you were right, it's the best fuck I've ever had. I've never had such a big dick in me, and I thought

I was big, and no-one has ever milked my cock like your ass did," he said, squeezing Hans's hand. Hans felt honoured by this compliment and squeezed back. Mike then rose to his feet, opened the door and said, "Should we go and have a shower and clean up?"

The three of them headed towards the showers. Hans and Jeff moved into one of the shower cubicles, while Mike went into one by himself. What went on in Jeff's cubicle, Mike didn't know, but he was happy to let the water pour over his tired body.

The water splashed onto the floor and the steam rose as Mike stood in the shower letting his whole body relax. He turned his back on the entrance to his cubicle and faced the tap. He turned the cold water down a bit and let the hot water run over his head. When he had had enough, he turned the water off and turned around. While he had his back turned, a guy had walked into the cubicle opposite his. Mike stood in the cubicle letting the remainder of the water drip from his body, staring at the guy opposite him.

The guy facing Mike, had a moustache, short hair, was built like a body-builder, about six feet tall and had a long uncut cock hanging between his legs. He stood with his legs apart, soaping his body and letting the soap run over his chest, stomach, cock and legs.

He stared at Mike and let his hand run across his chest, down his stomach and onto his cock, which he pulled. He then lifted his arms to get the soap off of them. Mike saw his muscles flex as he rubbed the soap from him. He turned slightly and stretched a leg out so that the water could run down it and wash the soap off. The legs were toned and muscular. He then turned his back on Mike. Mike could feel his cock beginning to swell as his thoughts centered on the body-builder. The guy flexed his ass muscles, creating a beautiful sight for Mike. He then continued turning until he was once again facing Mike; but this time when he faced Mike, his long cock was no longer limp. It now protruded straight ahead of him. He ran his hand over its length, still staring at Mike. He took the soap, lathered it and again rubbed his soap-coated hand over his cock. As he did so, he pulled his foreskin as far back as it would go. Mike immediately thought of Hans and how he had enjoyed sucking Hans's uncut cock, and this caused his own cock to spring to attention.

The body-builder had a slight smile on his face when he saw Mike's reaction, but continued to play with his dick. He motioned for Mike to come across and join him in the shower, which Mike did. Mike stretched out his hand when he got there, not to shake hands, but to take hold of this guy's cock.

"What's your name?" asked the body-builder.

"Mike, and yours?"

"Pierre. I'm on holiday from Paris."

"You've got a beautiful body," said Mike. "It's so well defined. Obviously you work out a lot at gym."

"Thank you, but you too have a sexy body," he replied in his broken English.

"I don't think it's sexy," replied Mike. "I've just got this from being a construction worker."

"You should work out at gym and you too could look even better." He pulled Mike closer to him. "You have a big dick and a cute ass," said Pierre.

"Thanks," said Mike, " so have you."

"I saw you looking at my muscles," said Pierre, flexing his arms. "Would you like to feel them?"

Mike stretched out a hand to feel Pierre's arms. As he did so, both their erect dicks rubbed against each other.

"Those are so hard," said Mike. "How long did it take you to get your body like this?"

"Oh a long time of hard work," replied Pierre. "Are there any other muscles you would like to feel?" he asked wryly.

Mike didn't need an invitation like this. His hand went down and held onto Pierre's dick.

"That's also so hard," said Mike, looking deep into Pierre's eyes and not letting go.

Pierre stretched his hand to Mike's cock, felt its hardness and said, "You too have a hard muscle like me. Would you like mine?"

"In what way do you mean," asked Mike.

"I think you have a nice ass," said Pierre. "Would you like me to slip my cock in there?"

Mike thought about it for a while before answering. He was like Jeff, not really into being fucked, but he had done it before, if he liked the guy.

"Yes, I would," said Mike.

Mike slid down the wet body of Pierre until he reached the tip of his dick. He held Pierre's dick and nibbled at his foreskin. Pierre's head was thrown back and the water gushed over their bodies. Mike then slipped his tongue under the hood of Pierre's foreskin and let it encircle his cock-head. Pierre gave a gentle groan of approval. Mike then slipped his mouth over Pierre's dick and slid it down his throat. He pulled up to the tip again, and once more nibbled the tip. Pierre was enjoying this.

"You know how to please a man!"

"I like to please," said Mike returning to his actions again.

While he was doing this, he occasionally looked up and saw Pierre playing with his nipples, squeezing and tweaking them.

Mike moved in between Pierre's legs and licked the insides of them, working his way up to Pierre's balls. When he reached them, he gently sucked one and then the other, creating a sensational feeling in Pierre's groin area. This continued for some time and then Pierre took Mike by the shoulders and lifted him up so that they were face to face.

Pierre opened his mouth as an invitation for Mike's tongue to explore inside. When Mike's tongue entered Pierre's mouth, he sighed and said, "You taste good."

"It's not me that tastes good, it's you," replied Mike. "I love the taste of your dick."

Pierre smiled at him and said, "You haven't tasted my dick yet. When I slide it into you, then you will taste it."

Mike moved his mouth to Pierre's nipples and started nibbling them. Pierre gave out a loud cry of ecstasy.

"Harder, make them harder," he said, thrusting his pecs into Mike's face. "Eat them!"

Mike wrapped his mouth around one and sucked on Pierre's nipple. He was writhing with pleasure, and as he did so, he was playing with his dick.

"I must have you," said Pierre, turning Mike's back towards him.

Mike bent slightly to make Pierre's entry a little more comfortable for him.

Pierre took his stiff cock, pulled his foreskin as far back as it would go, aimed for Mike's entrance and slowly pushed forward. Mike met his push and backed onto Pierre's cock.

Mike let out a low growl as he did so until Pierre was embedded in him right up to his balls. Pierre held his position for a while, because without saying so to Mike, Mike's ass had tightened around his cock and was creating a pressure on it, which might cause him to come before anything had really happened.

When Pierre had gained control, he slowly started his rhythmic penetration of Mike's ass. Both men worked at their action pushing and thrusting to meet each other. Mike was enjoying this as he felt the strong muscular arms around his waist working on his cock, and the long, hard cock rubbing up against his prostate. He ground his ass tightly against Pierre, which made Pierre thrust even deeper. While Pierre pounded at Mike's ass, Mike twisted his upper body so that he could gain access to Pierre's nipples. He pinched them and as he did so, Pierre thrust forward with all his might. The more

Mike played with Pierre's nipples, the more the man got worked up until he couldn't contain himself any longer and Mike felt a warm flood entering him. Pierre's breathing was heavy and rapid as he shot load after load into Mike. Mike ground harder onto Pierre's cock and squeezed his balls. Mike could feel himself nearing his climax. As he came, he thrust backwards, embedding Pierre's cock firmly in his ass and sprayed his hot cum over Pierre's hand, which had been working on Mike's dick. When Mike had finished shooting his load, and his body had become more relaxed, Pierre raised his cum covered hand to Mike who took his fingers into his mouth and sucked on them just the same way that he had sucked on Pierre's cock, earlier.

The two men stood under the pouring water in each other's arms and let the warmth of the water and their bodily warmth, caress them. Pierre said to Mike, "you really have a great ass," patting it gently.

"Thanks, Pierre, but so have you, and I wouldn't mind getting into that sometime."

"Maybe," he said with a grin, "we'll see."

They switched the shower off and went into the drying area to dry themselves.

"Are you staying in Amsterdam for long?" asked Mike, wrapping the towel around his now dry body.

"No, I leave tomorrow for Paris," replied Pierre. "Have you ever been to Paris?"

"No, this is my first trip overseas," replied Mike, "but I'm planning to see as much of Europe as I can."

"When are you leaving Amsterdam?" asked Pierre.

"I've got no time constraints," said Mike, "I can come and go as I please."

"So why don't you come with me and I'll show you Paris. Are you alone?"

"Yes," answered Mike.

"You do not have a partner?" queried Pierre.

Mike shook his head.

"Mon dieu! I cannot believe that someone as good looking and strong as you does not have a man in his life! However, you are more than welcome to stay at my home," said Pierre.

"That's very kind of you, Pierre, but I don't like to be a burden to anyone."

"You will not be a burden, besides, didn't you say you wanted to get into my ass sometime? If you don't come with me, you'll never get to see it again." Pierre smiled a mischievous smile and winked at Mike.

"So long as you really don't mind."

"Where are you staying in Amsterdam?" Pierre asked.

"Close by," said Mike, in a small hotel.

"It's not by any chance in Leidsekruisstraat?" asked Pierre.

Mike laughed, "Yes how did you know?"

"Because I am staying there as well."

Both men laughed at the co-incidence.

"Are you staying on here at the sauna or are you going anywhere else tonight?" asked Mike, "because I'm going back to the hotel."

"No, I think I'll also go back to the hotel," said Pierre.

As the two men walked back to their hotel, they discussed what they were going to do the next day, what time they were going to leave for Paris, and Pierre told Mike of all the exciting things they could do once they got to France.

When they arrived at the hotel, Mike had a surprise waiting for him.

"Hi Uncle Mike. Have you been out enjoying what the city has to offer?"

"Barry! What are you doing here?" asked Mike, somewhat bewildered by his nephew's sudden appearance.

"Mum got me onto an earlier flight as I was driving her insane with my persistence to come over and meet you, so here I am."

Mike was thrown by Barry's sudden appearance.

"Are you staying here at the hotel?" asked Mike.

"I told the receptionist that I was your nephew. He looked kinda strangely at me, but said I could stay in your room and wait for you."

Mike smiled and wondered what had gone through Hans's mind when Barry had arrived. Maybe he thought that Mike had found another guy to spend the night with! Mike said goodnight to Pierre and told him he'd meet him in the morning, and he and Barry went up to his room.

When they arrived in Mike's room, a thought suddenly struck him; if he had agreed to stay with Pierre in Paris, what was he going to do about Barry? He couldn't expect his young nephew to stay somewhere else as he'd promised his sister that he'd look after the young guy.

"Barry, make yourself comfortable while I just nip downstairs for a minute."

Mike hurried down to reception to find out what room Pierre was in, found out and headed to the room. He knocked on Pierre's door. The door opened and a naked Pierre stood in the doorway.

"This is a nice surprise," said Pierre, grinning at Mike.

"Sorry to disturb you Pierre, but I have a slight problem. As you know my nephew has just arrived from the States and he's going to be traveling with me, so I don't know if I can take up your offer of accommodation in Paris."

"You are both welcome to stay with me," replied Pierre. "He seems a nice young man."

"I appreciate that, but he's not gay or into guys, as far as I know."

Pierre laughed out loudly.

"Are you worrying that I might corrupt him?"

"Not at all, but I just thought I'd better let you know. He knows that I am gay, but I don't want to flaunt it in his face."

Again Pierre smiled to Mike.

"We shall be discreet."

"Thanks, Pierre," said Mike, closing the bedroom door and heading back up to his room.

When he reached his room, he found Barry lying on the double bed in his skimpy briefs, having just come out of the shower.

"I'm glad to see you've made yourself comfortable."

"Well you did tell me to," replied Barry.

There was no doubt in Mike's mind, his nephew had killer looks and a fine young body, the sort of physique that would attract attention. Barry was tall like his uncle and spent much time visiting his local gym to buff up his body. His dark brown hair was slicked back from the shower and Mike noticed a very good looking bulge in the front of Barry's briefs.

"So what's happening?" asked Barry, stretching across the double bed.

"Did you see that guy I was with when I came into the hotel?"

"Sure."

"Well, he's from Paris and he's said that we can go and stay at his place while we're visiting Paris."

Barry smiled at Mike.

"What are you grinning at?"

Barry laughed.

"Did you meet him tonight?"

"Yes, he's staying here at the hotel as well."

"You know that's not what I meant," giggled Barry. "So have you been having a good time here?"

"Hm! Not bad," replied Mike, blushing slightly.

"And how many guys have you met? Any Italians yet? Mum's really worried you're going to bring an Italian or a Frenchman home with you."

"Well you can tell her we've just met a Frenchman, so we'll see how things go with him."

"Don't worry, I won't say a word to her," replied Barry, winking at his uncle. "So how are we going to sleep?"

"As there's only one bed, I should imagine we'll be sleeping together."

Barry immediately pulled down the sheets and slipped under them.

"Well are you going to stand there staring at me or are you getting in?"

Mike stripped off to his underwear and climbed in alongside of Barry.

"Now I don't want any nonsense from you in the night, understand!" said Mike, trying to sound authoritarian to his young nephew.

"I promise I won't touch you, provided you promise not to touch me," was the answer.

They laughed, switched off the bedroom light and snuggled down to sleep.

In the early hours of the morning Barry awoke to find Mike's arms around him. He didn't mind. He smiled at his sleeping uncle and gently stroked his sleeping head, but under the sheets, he could also feel the hard-on that his uncle had, but that too didn't bother him either.

They awoke and showered, but Barry said nothing to Mike about how he had found him early in the morning. They packed their bags and prepared to leave Amsterdam. Mike and Barry went down for breakfast and met Pierre in the dining room.

"Did you sleep well last night?" enquired Pierre.

"Well as best I could," responded Mike, "but it wasn't easy with this young man sharing the bed and pinching the sheets all night."

Barry looked aghast at his uncle's snide comment and wondered whether he should say something about his uncle's arms being around him in bed, but chose not to embarrass him. Pierre raised his eyebrows at this point as if to say he too didn't believe Mike's story, but chose not to say anything.

Later in the morning, they all booked out of the hotel, but Mike told Hans that as his return home flight left from Amsterdam, he would be back, but didn't know when and that they'd come back and stay at the hotel. The three men then headed to the railway station to catch the train to Paris.

PARIS

The train journey from Amsterdam to Paris was a pleasant one, passing through picturesque countryside, while Pierre, Mike and Barry relaxed, enjoying each other's company. The train pulled into Gare du Nord station and they caught a cab to Pierre's apartment, which was near the station in Rue Pajol. Mike was happy to drop his luggage and relax, but extremely excited to be in Paris with its wealth of culture. Pierre had a two-bedroom apartment, so he offered the spare room to Mike and Barry. In their room were two single beds, so Barry was relieved to know that he wouldn't have his horny uncle sharing his bed for another night.

Pierre offered Mike and Barry some coffee and they sat, together with a map of Paris, and planned what they were going to do.

"Don't you work or have to go to work?" enquired Mike.

"Oh yes," replied Pierre, "I start again tomorrow, but with the work I do, I can fit you into my schedule."

"What work do you do?" asked Barry.

"I work at a gym around the corner from here," said Pierre. "That is why I have the body," he laughed.

"That explains everything," said Mike.

"Would you like to come to the gym with me when I go, Mike? Maybe we can work on some of those muscles of yours," he said squeezing Mike's leg under the table.

"That depends."

"On what?" enquired Pierre.

Mike merely blushed, but he was sure that Pierre understood to what he was referring.

"Tonight, I am going to make dinner for you two, and then we will go for a drink at my local bar, and then, if the night is still young, you may do what you please," said Pierre.

"Gee, that sounds like a good idea, thanks Pierre."

"I must buy food for us, but you two go out and see the sights that Paris has to offer. You have a map so you shouldn't get lost."

As the train had arrived in the early afternoon, there wasn't much time to be had to sightsee, so Mike and Barry headed for the most obvious tourist attraction – the Eiffel Tower. The view from the second level viewing platform was stupendous and they were both astounded by the vastness of Paris laid out before them.

"I didn't realize Paris was such a spread out city," remarked Mike as he gazed around him.

They were so high up the tower that below them the people did in fact appear the size of ants. The traffic was flowing and although there was a haze over the city, the view was uplifting. Barry was beginning to enjoy his first real taste of Europe and was looking forward to exploring Paris.

That evening, Pierre busied himself in the kitchen preparing a delicious chicken dish for Mike and Barry, who excitedly related to Pierre what they had done that afternoon. Pierre found that he enjoyed the young boy's enthusiasm for his beloved city, but was also aware of what Mike had said about Barry, not being gay. They sat at the dining room table, drinking a good red wine, enjoying the meal and each other's company. At about 10.30 that evening, the three guys dressed and left the apartment heading for Pierre's local bar and their first taste of Parisian nightlife.

The vibe in the bar was loud, happy and boisterous. People were singing, talking, standing with their arms around others, and in general, everyone seemed to be having a really good time. There was a mixed clientele in the bar, so Mike thought that perhaps Barry might find himself a pretty French girl to charm. Pierre ordered some drinks for them and they found a corner where they could stand and have their drinks. Occasionally, Pierre would speak to someone, but Mike didn't understand the language so he never knew what was being said. One young guy came up to Pierre and kissed him on both cheeks, said something in French and smiled at Mike. Mike politely smiled back. When the young guy moved off, Mike turned to Pierre.

"What did he say?"

"Oh he was admiring you," replied Pierre, "but I told him you were not available."

"Thanks, but why did you say I wasn't available?"

"Because there are better ones than that. That one is just one of those queens who want to brag about who they went to bed with," said Pierre, screwing up his face as he said so.

Another young man, came up to Pierre, pointed at Mike, and said something in French. Both men looked at Mike, nodded and carried on talking in earnest in French. When the young man had left, Mike said, "Now I know from your looks that you were talking about me. So what that did that guy want?"

"He told me that you were good-looking and you had a very good body and that you should enter the competition at L'Arene."

"What competition, and what or where is L'Arene?" asked Mike.

"L'Arene is what we call a men's club. You know, where, as you say, anything goes," commented Pierre, dropping his voice so that Barry wouldn't hear him.

"So what is the competition?"

"Apparently there is to be a competition tomorrow night, and I think you would have a good chance of winning. Even if you don't, you will definitely have a good time. What do you think?"

"I'm not entering anything that I know nothing about," said Mike.

"Trust me on this," laughed Pierre. "You're here for a good time, aren't you?"

"Sure."

"So, then don't worry."

"But what about Barry?" asked Mike.

Pierre shrugged his shoulders and sighed.

"Mon Amie, I do not know if he would like what happens there."

Mike was curious about the planned evening, but he also didn't want to neglect Barry, so he decided that he would speak to Barry and suggest that they go separate ways the following evening.

At midnight, they finished their drinks and Pierre said that as he had to get up early for work at the gym the following morning, so he was going home. Mike agreed, and so the three of them got a cab back to the apartment.

The following day, when Mike awoke, Pierre had already left for the gym and Barry was still asleep in bed. He rose and went into the kitchen where he made himself some coffee. As he sat drinking his coffee and listening to the early morning traffic, he looked from the lounge window to a view of the Eiffel Tower.

A little later the front door opened and in came Pierre. He was dressed in a white vest and a pair of Lycra shorts.

"Hi there," greeted Mike. "You're looking good this morning."

"Thanks Mike, but these are my usual working clothes, if that is what you are referring to."

"I've just made some coffee, would you like some, Pierre?"

"Thanks, but I think I need a shower first and get out of these sweaty clothes," said Pierre pulling his vest over his head to reveal a wet, sweaty, smooth chest.

Mike looked admiringly at Pierre's smooth body. His eyes moved down to Pierre's Lycra shorts and could see the outline of Pierre's big dick, resting peacefully.

"Have you had anything to eat, yet?" asked Pierre.

"No," replied Mike, "I was waiting for you, and it looks as if breakfast has arrived," he answered with a smirk on his face.

Mike was sitting only in a pair of briefs and he let his hand run over the front of them. Pierre smiled and watched him stroke the outline of his length.

"Do you want to eat now?" said Pierre with a glint in his eyes.

"Now is a good time," said Mike.

"Where's Barry?" asked Pierre.

"Still sleeping," answered Mike.

Pierre smiled again and walked over to where Mike was sitting and stood astride Mike's legs.

Mike rubbed the bulge in Pierre's shorts and could see Pierre's cock stir into life. He ran his tongue over its length, which was covered by the Lycra material, and could see that Pierre's cock was growing in both length and girth rapidly. In fact, Pierre's cock was beginning to strain to get out of his shorts. Mike pulled the top of Pierre's Lycra shorts down a little until he could see the top of Pierre's cock sticking out. He started to nibble at Pierre's foreskin. He bit on it and pulled it with his teeth. He looked up at Pierre and saw the expression of one who was almost in another world. He pulled the shorts down to Pierre's knees and his throbbing cock sprung out of its protective covering. Pierre's cock-head gleamed in the morning light as Mike salivated over it. Mike held Pierre's cock in his mouth and with his hand, began jerking Pierre off.

Mike removed his mouth from Pierre's cock and said, "When you do come, Pierre, I want you to come over my chest. I want to feel your warm cum running down my chest." Once he had informed Pierre of his request, he went back to using his mouth on Pierre's full length. Finally, Pierre thrust forward and gave a cry to warn Mike that he was about to come, pulled his cock from Mike's mouth and Mike frantically jerked him off. Pierre shot load after load onto Mike's chest and as he did so, Mike, using his free hand, rubbed it all over his chest and stomach. When Pierre was finished, he bent over to kiss Mike, took him by the hand and led him to the shower so that they could both clean up.

"I hope you enjoyed your breakfast," said Pierre taking Mike by the hand and leading him to the bathroom where he turned on the hot water tap of the shower and lead Mike under the pouring water.

"I think that should keep me going for a little while," said Mike, "but we'll see."

When they had finished showering, they dressed and at about the same time, Barry appeared.

"Hi guys," said Barry, looking sprightly and ready for a day's action. "What's happening?"

Mike and Pierre glanced at each other, wondering whether Barry had known what they'd been doing.

"I'm taking your uncle shopping," replied Pierre, casually.

"Does anybody mind if I do my own thing today?" asked Barry.

Excitedly, Mike answered, "Not at all. You go and enjoy yourself. Just write down Pierre's address and phone number in case you get lost."

Barry made himself something to eat while Mike and Pierre set off to do some shopping.

Pierre said to Mike, "Do you have a plain white T-shirt?" as they traveled on the Metro underground.

"Sure I do," replied Mike. "Why?"

"For tonight," came the reply. "Do you have some sexy underwear?"

"Pierre, what is this that you're going on about?"

"It's all for tonight."

"But what's happening tonight? If you don't tell me, I'm not going," said Mike.

"Are you trying to blackmail me?" laughed Pierre, "because if you are, it won't work. I am not saying anything more about it."

"What do you call sexy?" asked Mike.

"Well I wouldn't call big baggy shorts sexy. I thought more in line with what sexy Frenchmen wear."

"And what would a sexy Frenchman wear?" mocked Mike.

"Either a G-string or a bikini brief."

"Well I've got a bikini brief," said Mike, "but I'm afraid I don't have a G-string."

"Fine, then we'll buy you one. Do you also, by any chance, have any leather gear?"

"Actually I do. I bought some in London. Why?"

"Then wear some leather over your sexy underwear," replied Pierre.

They arrived at their destination, alighted from the train and Pierre marched off to a men's clothing shop with Mike in tow.

They entered the shop and Pierre explained to the shop assistant what he wanted and that it was not for him but for his friend. The assistant brought out about four G-strings of varying size. Pierre picked them up one at a time and surveyed them.

"This one is far too small for you," he said, throwing the G-string on to the counter. "Maybe this could fit you, but I'm not sure about the colour. Mike, do you like tropical green?"

"It doesn't look too bad to me," said Mike, picking up one of the other G-strings.

"Do you like that one?"

"Hm, I think so."

Mike held the canary yellow G-string in front of him.

"I think we need a bigger size," said Pierre.

The assistant said something in French to Pierre who snapped a reply back and looked sternly at the sales assistant. The assistant scuttled off and returned with a number of yellow G-strings in different sizes.

"He doesn't believe that this one is too small for you," said Pierre, holding up a G-string, " but I should know."

The assistant then led Mike to a changing cubicle to try on the garments.

Mike peeled off his shorts and pulled on the first G-string. Pierre, who was standing in the change cubicle made Mike turn around while he checked the garment's appearance.

"Take it off, it's too small."

"What do you mean too small, I think it fits well," said Mike.

"Take it off," commanded Pierre.

When the assistant heard this, he came nearer to the cubicle to listen. He gently pulled part of the curtain apart and saw Mike standing naked with his back to him.

"Try this one on," said Pierre, handing Mike another G-string. Mike obliged.

As Mike turned around he saw the assistant's face peeping through the curtain. He smiled and said, "What do you think? Do you think that this one is OK?"

Pierre turned to see who Mike was talking to and saw the assistant.

"Mon dieu," said the assistant, "it is so big."

"Do you mean the G-string or what's inside it?" asked Pierre, sarcastically.

This immediately caused the assistant to disappear. Both guys laughed at the hurried exit and resumed their task of finding the right garment.

"This actually feels too big," said Mike.

"Then we take it," said Pierre. "If it is loose, it allows your cock to hang freely, but if it is too tight, your cock will be constricted."

"What difference does it make?" asked Mike.

"You will see that I am right, tonight."

They paid for the garment and left the shop and the assistant who was busily explaining to his colleagues what a sight he had just seen.

Back at the apartment Pierre explained to Mike what he was to wear that evening and while they prepared for the evening's event, they chatted about how Mike was enjoying his French hospitality.

"I think Barry is enjoying himself here," said Mike. "And I'm glad he's out doing his own thing. I had visions of having to look after him all the time."

"If he is not back by the time we leave, we can leave a note for him," suggested Pierre.

That evening, Barry had not yet returned, so Pierre and Mike ate a light dinner together, dressed and set off for the club. Mike was wearing his bright yellow G-string, his new tight leather jeans, a white T-shirt with a loose fitting shirt, which was left unbuttoned over the T-shirt. Pierre, on the other hand, wore a tight, cropped T-shirt, which revealed his muscular torso, and a pair of Lycra shorts, which revealed his bulging cock and muscular legs.

"You look as if you are hoping to pick something up tonight," joked Mike, on seeing Pierre's attire.

"Hopefully, I will," joked Pierre, posing for Mike.

They caught a cab and after a short drive, soon arrived at the club. A neon sign announced the L'Arene Club. They went in and Mike's eyes widened when he saw the people there. Most of the people he could see were flaunting their bodies and had every right to do so. He couldn't remember having ever been in a room with so many half naked, muscular looking men. Pierre took him by the arm and led him over to the bar. Pierre spoke in French to the barman who then smiled at Mike and said in English, "Welcome to our club. We hope that you have a good time."

"Thanks," said Mike. "Pierre, what sort of club is this that there are so many well-built buys here?"

"I told you it was a men's club. These are men, not like the people you saw last night."

The club was crowded and the mood was festive. Music was blaring and the drinks were flowing. People were dancing, some were kissing and then Pierre said,

"Would you like to have a look around?"

"You mean there are things to see?"

"Follow me," was all Pierre said.

They left the main club area, walked down a passage and turned left into a room where a video machine was playing porno films, and a number of people were busy entangled in other people's arms and legs. Mike surveyed the scene and then Pierre took his arm again and led him out of the room before he had a chance to consider joining in with the action. They continued down the passage and then down a flight of steps. When they reached the bottom, they found themselves in a large open room with three slings hanging from the ceiling, some racks against one of the walls, clamps on another wall, and lying on a table were a number of sex toys, such as whips and dildos.

In one of the slings lay a guy with his legs in the air, busy being fucked by someone, while another had his dick in the young guy's mouth. Pierre walked over to the three men, but never said anything. He stood alongside the guy in the sling who stretched out a hand to rub along the length of Pierre's shaft. The sling was swaying backwards and forwards, causing the fucker to penetrate deeply into the young guy's ass. Pierre's cock was becoming erect, but he didn't want to get involved in a scene yet, so he moved back to where Mike was standing.

"Didn't you want to join in?' asked Mike.

"Later," said Pierre, adjusting his swollen cock in his Lycra shorts. "The night's still young."

They climbed back up the steps and headed down the passage again. When they got to another doorway, Pierre paused.

"This is the dark room," he said. "If you want to have fun there without knowing who you're doing it with, this is the place to be in."

Mike tried to peer into the darkness, but couldn't see anything.

By the time they reached the main club floor again, Mike noticed that in their absence, a fairly large plastic portable pool had been placed in the middle of the floor.

"What's the swimming pool for?" enquired Mike.

Pierre smiled a huge grin at him and said, "You!"

"What do you mean, me?"

"That's part of the competition," said Pierre. "It's a wet T-shirt and underwear competition."

"So why do you want me to enter? Look at all these beautiful bodies in this place. Look at your beautiful build."

"I've had my turn in this competition, now it's yours," said Pierre.

Suddenly the music stopped and an announcer told the thronging audience that the competition was about to begin and that all the entrants were to report to him. A trickle of men wandered over to the announcer. Pierre pushed Mike forward.

"Go on, this is your moment."

"I won't understand what they're saying," said Mike.

"I'll come with you," replied Pierre.

When Pierre got to the announcer, he said something in French and when the announcer saw Mike and had heard Pierre, he broke into English.

"Gentlemen, we have a tourist among us who is entering the competition and whose French is not so good, so I will announce in English," said the announcer.

He turned to the contestants and said, "Guys, the rules are simple: You may only wear a T-shirt and your underwear; you may not have anything stuffed into your underwear, except your cocks; and where possible, we would like your cocks to remain slack. Any questions?"

"In what order are we going?" asked a young blonde giant.

"We draw lots," said the announcer. "Each of you will be given a number and when I draw your number, then you will have to come forward."

All the contestants took off their clothes and handed them to friends to keep. Mike handed his shirt and leather jeans to Pierre and then he, as well as the rest of the audience, stood staring at the contestants. There were tall men and short ones, well built and medium built, big cocks and bigger cocks.

Mike turned to the blonde giant. "I'm sorry, but what do we have to do?"

"All you do is climb into the swimming pool, wet yourself from head to toe, climb out and parade in front of the audience and the judges," replied the quietly spoken young man.

"Thanks," said Mike. "Have you done this before?"

"Oh yes, two or three times, but I have never won."

The contestants were given their numbers and waited for the announcer to shout the order.

"Number seven," shouted the announcer.

A tall, athletic man walked forward, wearing a pair of boxer shorts and climbed into the water in the pool. He submerged himself in the water; rose to the surface again and then exited the pool. His T-shirt clung to his chest and so did his boxer shorts, but they didn't do much to enhance his equipment. He paraded in front of the audience who applauded and whistled their approval.

"Number one," shouted the announcer, again.

A short, stocky guy with a balding head stepped forward. He climbed into the water, covered himself with water and climbed out again. The audience went wild with enthusiasm as his T-shirt clung tightly to his muscular chest. Through his wet, white bikini briefs, one could see a large, cut dick. He too paraded in front of the audience to thunderous applause.

Each contestant, in turn, went through the motions of getting wet and parading.

"Number four!"

The blonde giant, who had been standing next to Mike, talking to him, stepped forward. As he walked towards the pool, one could see his dick bouncing in his briefs. He entered the water, lowered his body under it, resurfaced and stepped out of the pool. Mike could see that the guy was well-endowed and had a beautifully defined body. The noise from the cheering audience was deafening. They applauded, cheered, whistled and shouted their approval. He walked slowly past the judges and the audience, his cut cock bouncing in his pale yellow briefs as he walked. Mike was taken by what he saw.

"Number five!"

Mike hesitated. He looked towards where Pierre was standing and saw him smiling at him. Pierre nodded his head as if to say, "Go for it." Mike moved forward to the pool.

The water was warm. He looked across at the blonde giant and saw his huge cock in his wet briefs. Mike's mind went into action and he could feel the start of an erection coming. He submerged his whole body in the water, rose again and climbed out of the pool. When the audience saw his ten-inch, cut cock hanging in his bright yellow G-string, they went absolutely crazy. They jumped into the air, shouted, cheered, whistled and basically went mad with excitement. Even the blonde giant stared in disbelief and applauded. Pierre was ecstatic.

Mike walked past the judges and smiled sweetly at them. Nobody in the audience seemed to worry that he was not as well built as some of the other contestants, but when it came to size, there was no one to touch him. Mike went and stood next to his blonde friend while the judges concurred.

"Fuck, but you're hung," said the blonde, still staring at Mike's cock. "How big does that thing get when you've got a hard-on?"

Mike laughed embarrassedly, and said casually, "Only a little bit bigger."

The announcer tapped the microphone.

"Gentlemen, the judges are ready."

One of the judges handed him a piece of paper, which the announcer opened.

"In third place, number one."

There were cheers all around as the stocky guy went up to the announcer. They shook hands and he was presented with a check and a bottle of champagne.

"In second place, number four."

Mike patted his blonde friend on the back and said, "Well done."

The blonde giant eased his way up to the announcer, his cock bouncing in his still wet briefs. He too shook hands and was given his prizes. He stood there smiling at the audience and enjoying his moment of glory, holding his bottle of champagne. He looked towards Mike, smiling, and as he did so, he rubbed the bottle over his huge cock. Mike's cock reacted when he saw this and he could feel his cock getting harder. He stood with his hands in front of him to try and hide the erection that was forming.

"And our winner for this year is, number five."

The club erupted with approval. Mike remained a little stunned at first and then streamers were thrown over Mike and everyone was patting him on the back. Suddenly he realized that he was the winner. He was pushed forward by the crowd and as he went forward his hands moved away from his raging hard-on. When the audience saw his throbbing cock standing erect in his G-string, everyone cheered and whistled. Mike looked embarrassed as he neared the announcer, but nobody seemed to mind, especially seeing that what they saw was a beautiful sight. Pierre cheered loudly. When Mike received his prize, which was a check for five hundred Euros, a bottle of champagne and a trophy shaped like a cock, the blonde guy came forward and hugged Mike. They both felt the other's thick cock pressing against each other. The blonde kissed Mike on the lips and the club cheered.

"You deserved that," said the blonde.

"Thanks," said Mike, who was now enjoying the moment, "but I think you really deserved it. You've got a much better body than I have."

"But you've got a much bigger cock than I have," said the blonde.

Pierre interrupted them as he flung his arms around Mike.

"I told you, I told you," repeated Pierre. "I told you a loose G-string wouldn't constrict your cock and therefore you could let it all hang out, if you know what I mean."

The manager of the club came forward and presented each of the winners with a gold sash, which they had obviously forgotten to present to them while they were on stage.

The stocky guy went off with his friends while Mike, Pierre and the blonde stood chatting together. Pierre turned to Mike and said, "Mike, let me introduce you to a friend of mine. Mike, this is Eric," he said, pointing to the blonde giant.

"Do you know everybody?" asked Mike.

"Only those who mean something to me," said Pierre. "Many years ago in Germany, Eric and I had a relationship together, but after we broke up, we remained good friends, not so?" he said, slapping Eric's ass.

"I'm very pleased to meet you Eric," said Mike.

Pierre leaned close to Mike's ear and whispered into it, "What do you think of him?"

Eric obviously heard what was said because he smiled at Mike and winked.

Mike decided to play along with Pierre and leaned towards Pierre's ear and whispered, but loud enough for Eric to hear, "I think he's very cute."

Eric blushed and felt his cock stir in his briefs.

Mike continued. "And I think he's got a cute ass and a very nice dick."

"I think so too," whispered Pierre. "Should we go somewhere?"

"Where?" asked Mike.

"Come with me," said Pierre as he moved off along the passage that led from the main club area.

Their bottles of champagne were left at the bar counter for safe keeping, then Mike put an arm around Eric's shoulder and the two followed Pierre. It was the most beautiful sight to see these two hunky guys with their heavily hung cocks bouncing as they walked. Pierre led them down the stairs into the dungeon where the slings were, and the two followed. When the two got there, there were no other people around, except for Pierre.

Pierre moved across to Eric, ran his fingers over his smooth chest and said, "Would you like to do it as we used to, but this time there will be three of us?"

Eric looked at Mike and then nodded his head. He pulled off his wet T-shirt and stepped out of his briefs. As he did so, his cock sprung free and started to rise into the air. He then crossed to one of the slings, lay on his back in it and lifted his legs into the air, resting them on the chains, which were attached to the roof.

"He is all yours, Mike," said Pierre. "I know you want him, so take him, he's yours to enjoy."

"But what about you?" asked Mike.

"I'll be here."

Mike moved to Eric's feet, smiled into Eric's eyes and then crouched between his legs. He licked Eric's ass entrance and spread his cheeks to try and get his tongue deeper into Eric. He ran his tongue over Eric's balls and sucked and nibbled on them. While he was doing this, Pierre watched, rubbing his hands over his ever-growing hard-on in his Lycra shorts. He moved towards Eric's face and stood as close to it as he could get. Eric's mouth rubbed over the length of Pierre's dick making his Lycra shorts wet from the saliva in his mouth.

Mike's mouth moved up onto Eric's swollen and throbbing cock. He licked it around the head and then placed his lips over it. Slowly he sank his mouth over its length. Eric let out a sigh of delight as Mike did this. Eric then pulled the waistband of Pierre's shorts down to reveal his uncut hard-on. Eric pulled Pierre's cock closer to his mouth. Pierre could feel Eric's warm breath against his cock. Eric opened his mouth and nibbled and chewed at Pierre's foreskin. Pierre thrust his cock forward hoping that Eric's mouth would take it all, but instead, Eric continued to chew.

Mike moved his ten inches closer to Eric's ass. He positioned it at the entrance and gently pushed forward. Eric felt this and prepared himself for the assault. Mike continued to push forward. His thick cock-head slowly pushed passed Eric's sphincter and then the long shaft continued the journey until he had sunk into the depths of Eric's ass. Eric had not made any sounds of pain, instead he merely moaned with pleasure. As Mike had his full length embedded in Eric, Eric opened his mouth and swallowed Pierre's cock. Mike held onto the chains supporting the sling and looked at Eric's face, which was a picture of pure contentment. Mike started a slow rhythmic movement, which caused the sling to sway backwards and forwards. As Mike's cock slid into Eric, it would push the sling away from him, causing Eric's mouth to go further over the length of Pierre's cock.

Mike stretched across Eric's body to take hold of Pierre's nipples. He pulled on his nipples, forcing Pierre to move closer in. Mike's actions had increased in speed and he was now holding onto Eric's hips, pulling him closer onto his cock, forcing it deeper into Eric's ass. Eric was slurping loudly on Pierre's cock and Pierre was beginning to pound his cock harder into Eric's mouth. The sling was now swaying ferociously as the two men assaulted Eric's ass and mouth. Eric was meeting each thrust from Mike, and was sucking as hard as he could on Pierre. He knew that Pierre was close and so he worked his tongue round the head of Pierre's cock. Mike in the meantime still held onto Pierre's nipples and was pinching them hard. Pierre was groaning in agony as Mike worked on his nipples and Eric worked on his cock. He gave a cry and shot his warm cum into Eric's mouth. Eric worked furiously on Pierre's cock, sucking and swallowing and fast as he could. Mike pounded harder to try and come. Eric held Pierre's cock in his mouth for some time, milking it dry, then Pierre slowly pulled his subsiding cock from Eric's mouth and moved around to the side of Eric. He bent over Eric and took Eric's throbbing cock into his mouth and sank over it taking its full length down his throat. As Eric felt his cock-head hit the back of Pierre's throat, he couldn't contain himself any longer and cried out as his hot cum passed down Pierre's open throat. Pierre never moved his mouth, but let the cum shoot down the back of his throat.

As Eric shot his first load, his ass muscles clamped tightly around Mike's cock giving him a great sensation. Mike's breathing had become much heavier and his fucking more frantic. Suddenly he tensed and gave a long, low growl. His balls rose up against the base of his dick and the first of a number of shots were fired into Eric's waiting ass. He pulled Eric further onto his cock, embedding it deeply into Eric's ass. When he had emptied himself, he gently pulled out of Eric, allowed him to lower his legs and moved around to his side where he leaned over and kissed him. Mike and Pierre helped Eric from the sling; they put their clothes back on and went up the stairs to join the others in the club celebrating their friendship and their success. They danced with each other, partied and thoroughly enjoyed the evening.

"Are you glad I told you about the competition?" asked Pierre.

"Sure thing," said Mike. "I don't know what I'm going to say to people when they see my prize, but more than that I'm glad that I met Eric tonight."

"And I'm glad I met you, Mike," said Eric. "Are you staying in Paris for long?"

"I don't know, that's up to Pierre and my nephew, who I presume is out enjoying himself somewhere in Paris as we speak. However, when I do leave, I'm hoping to go to Berlin."

"Berlin! That's where my brother stays," said Eric. "If you like, I can give you his address, in case you have nowhere to stay."

"Thanks Eric, that would be nice, but is he as good looking as you?"

"Better, he's only nineteen so he's still got his looks."

"What does he do, Eric?" asked Mike.

"He's a model."

"That's putting it mildly," joked Pierre.

"What do you mean, Pierre?" asked Mike.

"Oh he models all right, but not in the way you might think."

"You're just jealous," laughed Eric.

"So what does he actually do?" said Mike.

"He's a porn star," said Eric.

"A Porn Star!" exclaimed Mike, not quite sure whether he should believe it or not.

Both Pierre and Eric were laughing loud as they looked at Mike's facial reaction.

"You're having me on," said Mike. "I don't believe you."

"I tell you what," said Eric, " when you get to Berlin, give him a call and ask him."

Mike didn't say anything to the guys but he suddenly had mixed feelings. He had never been with a porn star before and one half of him was saying that this could be exciting, but the other half was saying, no, don't do it.

"I'll tell you what, if I have time, I'll give him a call," said Mike.

Pierre invited Eric to stay the night at his apartment with himself and Mike; so the three of them left the club after having a most enjoyable evening, and went back to the flat where they spent the night making love to each other in Pierre's double bed.

During the night, the telephone in Pierre's apartment rang but because the three guys were busy in bed, nobody answered it. It stopped ringing and went into answering mode.

The following morning when Mike awoke, he went in to his room and noticed that Barry's bed had not been slept in, so he became a little concerned that he might have got lost or got into trouble.

"Pierre, I'm very worried about Barry," said Mike, waking up his host. "Barry never slept in his bed last night and I don't know where he is."

Pierre yawned, stretched and said, "Do not trouble your little heart.

I'm sure that he'll be fine. Maybe he met someone nice and stayed the night at her house."

"It's just not like him," replied Mike, concern in his voice.

Pierre climbed out of bed, leaving Eric still sleeping, and padded through to the kitchen to make some coffee. As he did so, so he switched on the answering machine to his phone. A stressed and agitated English speaking voice came over the machine. Pierre listened intently, rewound the machine's tape to listen again, then shouted for Mike.

"Mike come here to the lounge and listen to this."

Mike did as he was asked and the two men listened to the recording. While they were doing so, Eric came into the lounge to join them.

"What's the problem?" asked Eric.

Both Pierre and Mike were dumbstruck by what they heard: Barry had been kidnapped.

"Who and why would anyone want to kidnap Barry?" asked Mike, trying to make some sense out of the situation. "And what do we do?"

Mike's mind flashed to his family back home and how he was going to have to explain to them what had happened.

"We contact the police," suggested Pierre, who could see how upset Mike was becoming.

He immediately dialed a number and, speaking in French, explained the situation, and then when he'd completed telling the police, he allowed Mike to put through a call to the United States to his family.

Within half an hour, the French police had arrived at Pierre's apartment and were taking down notes. One of the messages on the answering machine stated that the kidnappers would call back to tell them what their demands were. The police immediately decided to set up a system whereby they would be able to trace all calls made to Pierre's phone. As there were no clues in the message that had been left on Pierre's phone, as to the whereabouts of Barry, the police decided to wait for the ransom call to be made.

Eric had to get to work, so he left but Pierre phoned the gym and told them that he wouldn't be in to work that day. Instead, he stayed at his apartment all day with Mike, waiting for any phone call from the kidnappers.

Neither Mike nor Pierre could understand why anyone would kidnap Barry. He was an innocent tourist; not from a wealthy family or some industrialist's family. Nothing seemed to make sense, especially to Mike.

After a whole day of waiting, at approximately four in the afternoon, Pierre's telephone rang. The police were waiting to see if they could trace the call. On the police's signal, Pierre picked up the telephone and a Germanic sounding voice was on the other end of the line.

"You will listen, and listen carefully if you want your friend to live," said the voice. "We want two million Euros in used notes. You have until midnight to get the money otherwise we will kill him."

"What must I do with the money?" asked Pierre, trying to play for time to help the police to trace the call.

"We will phone again at 22:00 to tell you where to place the money."

The phone went dead.

The police looked solemn, knowing that the dialogue was too short for them to trace the call.

When Pierre told Mike what had been said on the phone, Mike was astounded at the amount of the ransom. He couldn't get that sort of money, nor could he understand why that amount. It wasn't that Barry wasn't worth that amount of money, but Mike couldn't come to terms with the whole episode. Somehow he could understand if Barry came from a very wealthy family, but his family was just like any other ordinary family.

"Nothing makes sense, Pierre, but where am I going to get that sort of money from? Neither I nor Barry is from a wealthy family. I'm sure that this is all some terrible mistake and perhaps they've taken the wrong person."

The policeman manning the equipment trying to trace the call spoke up.

"Sir, this call didn't come from anywhere in Paris."

"What do you mean not from Paris?" questioned Pierre. "It must have been made somewhere here in Paris."

"No sir, that we are certain."

"Are you suggesting," asked Mike, "that they are out of the country?"

"Perhaps sir," replied the policeman. "If not the country, then they are out of Paris."

Again Mike was dumbstruck by this revelation. Pierre remained silent for a while, then he had a thought.

"I wonder if the call wasn't perhaps made from just across the border with Germany."

"What makes you say that, Pierre?" asked Mike.

"The Germanic voice. They could quite easily have kidnapped Barry and whipped him over the border into Germany to get him away from the prying eyes of the French police."

The policeman manning the equipment nodded his head in agreement.

"I hear what you say, but it could someone German who happens to live in France and not necessarily be over the border."

"So what do we do?" enquired Mike.

"Notify the German police," suggested Pierre. "In case they are in fact in Germany."

"What are we going to do about the money?" enquired Mike.

"What about involving the American Embassy," suggested Pierre. "I think they ought to be contacted because it involves a citizen of theirs and it is, after all an international situation."

Pierre looked up the American Embassy telephone number and eventually got put through to the ambassador, who listened intently to all the information being given to him. Once he had heard everything, he reassured Mike that everything would be done to get Barry back.

A representative of the embassy arrived at Pierre's apartment and spoke to the French police on duty there. He also spoke to Mike and Pierre, asking them if they had any idea why someone might want to kidnap Barry.

Naturally both men were still puzzled.

Later in the day, the embassy had arranged with a bank in Paris to get the two million Euros, but they suggested that the money not be handed over to the kidnappers until Barry had been safely returned to the police.

Mike's only concern was the safety of Barry.

"If anything happens to him, I'll die," he said to Pierre.

"Don't you worry. We'll get him back safely," reassured Pierre.

At 20:00, there was knock at the front door to Pierre's apartment. He went to open the door and when he did, he found no one there, but lying on the doorstep was a box. He hesitated before picking it up, then gently carried it into the lounge and handed it to the French police on duty. It was addressed to Mike.

The police gingerly opened the parcel, in case it had some destructive device attached to it, and when it was safely opened, handed its contents to Mike.

"A video!" exclaimed Mike.

"Quick, put it in my machine," said Pierre, taking the video from Mike and placing it in the video machine.

All turned to the TV set. A picture flickered onto the screen and then it became clearer. The scene resembled a bedroom, but it looked artificial. On the bed, strapped down to prevent his escape was Barry, who looked drugged. The lithe, young boy was naked. His muscular legs had been spread apart and had been hoisted up into the air, revealing his tight asshole. His arms were each attached to the bedstead and he was blindfolded. Everyone stared at the handsome young man lying motionless on the bed, and then the lower part of a person appeared on the screen, standing at the foot of the bed. It was clear that the person at the foot of the bed was also naked. A long, thick, erect uncut cock came into shot and Mike and Pierre instinctively knew where that huge cock was headed. Slowly the person's crotch neared Barry's waiting asshole. As the head of the person's cock touched Barry, he immediately tensed, although still in a drugged state, and so did Mike. He was standing watching his young nephew about to be raped.

Ever so slowly, the person pushed into Barry's tensed asshole and all the while the young boy was whimpering and writhing on the bed. Another pair of hands came into the shot and the viewers saw how the hands at first tried to prevent Barry from writhing and then they began to stroke Barry's now hardening cock. Mike watched with awe as his young nephew's cock began to grow in length and girth and he was impressed – the boy had been blessed with magnificent equipment. However, the act being committed brought dismay to Mike.

As the person at the foot of the bed's cock sank deeply into Barry, a sharp cry was emitted from Barry's lips and both Pierre and Mike shuddered. It was the cry of intense discomfort and they had heard those cries many times from men being penetrated. The slow, gentle insertion suddenly came to a halt and in its place came frantic thrusts deep into the chute of Barry. Barry continued to whimper as his attacker increased his pace and severity.

"Pause it!" shouted the French policeman who was also watching the rape.

The pause button was pressed and Barry and his attacker froze.

"What is it?" asked Mike.

"There in the background. I can make out part of a sign, but I do not know if it is significant."

Against a wall, in the background, and not in very large print, they could see the letters G–A–L, then Barry's raised leg got in the way, but after whatever the word was, they saw the word 'STUDIO'.

"That could be the name of a photographic studio," suggested Pierre.

Mike chose to look rather at the frozen picture of Barry. The guy screwing his nephew was well embedded in the young man's ass and the expression on Barry's face was one of traumatized pain. He felt for Barry and wished that he was there to save him from this punishment, but at the same time he had developed a hard-on, watching his nephew having sex with a man.

The policeman went closer to the TV screen to look at the picture. He wasn't looking at Barry, but beyond, in the background of the picture to see if he could find any other clues.

"I see a calendar in the background and can just make out something," said the policeman, pointing to the screen. "It is not clear, the name of the company, but in small print below it I can make out the word Berlin."

"Do you think that's where they might be?" asked Pierre, showing some excitement in the hopes that they had discovered Barry's whereabouts.

The tape was started up again and the rape of Barry continued, and so did his crying out in pain. Mike stood mesmerized, watching the deep thrusts going into Barry's tight, young ass. He glanced towards Pierre and noticed that he too was engrossed in the scene playing before them. Mike then glanced down at Pierre's crotch and noticed the swollen bulge there and he knew that his new friend was also finding the scene arousing.

Suddenly the scene was cut and a voice came over the tape saying, 'If you do not pay up, worse than this will happen to him.'

The policeman stopped the tape and removed it from the player and Pierre and Mike stood staring at each other, not knowing what to do.

"I think I've got to go to Berlin, Pierre. He must be being held there."

"But how are you going to find him. You don't know the city, nor do you know where to start looking."

"I need to look in the phone directory to see if there are any G-A-L Studios and take it from there," replied Mike.

At precisely 22:00, the telephone in Pierre's apartment rang shrilly, alerting all who were there that the time had arrived. Again Pierre answered the call on the instructions of the policeman.

"Have you got the money?" asked the Germanic voice.

"Not yet. We are having difficulty in getting the money at this time of the night," said Pierre, playing for time.

"You have until midnight, or your friend dies. We will phone again then to see if you have received the money and tell you where to place it. Did you get our present?"

"If you mean the video, yes. Now, I want to speak to the young man. Put him on the phone so that I know that he is still alive," demanded Pierre.

There was a slight pause as Mike and Pierre waited, then they heard the distinct voice of Barry.

"Uncle Mike, please help me," cried the young boy's voice.

Both Mike and Pierre shouted to Barry at the same time, "We'll get you, don't worry."

Then the Germanic voice was back.

"Remember you have until midnight."

Then the phone went dead once more.

The policeman operating the tape recorder that was recording the calls, played it back and listened intently.

"I can hear other voices in the background. It sounds like a room. They are definitely not phoning from a call box because there was no echo sound in the background, nor was there any sound of traffic," said the policeman. "And I think that it must be somewhere in Germany, because perhaps the calendar is the clue and that it's in Berlin."

Pierre suggested that if Mike did head to Berlin, that he might want to stay at a particular hotel that Pierre had found interesting, but they needed to wait for midnight to see what was going to happen.

The embassy official who had stayed with them in Pierre's apartment, offered to drive Mike to Berlin while Pierre and the French police remained at the apartment to take the phone calls. Mike agreed and hastily packed his suitcase and together with the official, they headed towards Germany. Pierre, in the meantime, waited for the midnight call.

As the car sped through the French countryside towards Germany, Mike sat in the passenger's seat thinking about his evening out in Paris and where he was now. He thought of Barry and how much his young nephew meant to him. Lush green countryside and rolling hills covered in vines flashed past, so did quaint villages, but Mike saw nothing of this, nor did the other occupant as they sped through the dark of the night towards Berlin.

At midnight in Paris, the telephone rang once more. The policeman switched on his tape recorder and nodded to Pierre to pick up the receiver.

"You have the money?" asked the voice.

"It has been arranged with the bank, but we won't be able to get it until tomorrow when the banks open," said Pierre, hoping that the kidnappers would buy his story and give Mike time to get to Berlin, provided that was where Barry was.

There was silence on the other end of the line, and then the voice spoke again.

"You have until midday tomorrow. The money is to be deposited in a Czech Republic bank account and here is the number. Write it down."

"OK, I'm ready," said Pierre, paper in front of him and pen in hand.

"204-4556-7900," said the voice. "Have you got that?"

Pierre repeated the number back to the voice, and then the line went dead. He replaced the phone and looked blankly at the policeman

"The Czech Republic! Why there, if the video showed Berlin?" muttered Pierre.

"Maybe I am wrong about the calendar and they are in the Czech Republic, but why have a German calendar on their wall," suggested the policeman.

"Don't say that, because Mike is already on his way to Berlin."

BERLIN

When Mike eventually arrived in Berlin, he and the embassy official went straight to the American Embassy in Berlin to report on the situation, and for them to inform the German police. However, the French police had already been in contact with their German counterparts and were able to inform Mike of the financial transaction that the kidnappers had requested.

"What we think you should do," remarked the Berlin embassy official, "is book into a hotel and wait for us to call you. There is nothing more that you can do. We think you must now leave everything to us and the German police."

Mike knew that he couldn't give up on Barry but took the advice of the embassy and caught a cab to the hotel in the Wittenbergplatz area, which Pierre had suggested.

He arrived at the hotel and booked into a clean, smartly furnished room. There were the usual hotel trappings, such as a TV, phone, shower and mini-bar in the room, but Mike also found out that the hotel featured a leather darkroom and offered massage services as well as workout facilities. No wonder Pierre had recommended it to him.

The first thing that Mike did once he'd booked in was to phone Pierre in Paris.

"Hi Pierre, it's Mike. Have you heard anything more about Barry?"

"Nothing as yet, my friend, but I believe your theory that they have the wrong person."

"Next time they phone, ask them the name of the person they have in captivity and I'm sure that they'll see they've made a mistake," suggested Mike.

"Listen my friend, you do what you have to in Berlin and I'll keep in touch with you, but if it's at all possible, enjoy yourself," said Pierre, hoping that Mike might go out and see the sights to take his mind off of the kidnapping. Pierre had also chosen not to say anything to Mike about the request for the money to be deposited in the Czech bank.

"Are you staying at the hotel I suggested?" enquired Pierre.

"Yes."

"Good, then I know where to contact you if I have to. Now don't worry too much, and go out and enjoy Berlin."

Mike took Pierre's advice and ventured out of the hotel, which was situated in the heart of the gay area, into the sunny street. The brightness of the sun seemed to warm and brighten him up a little. As Mike strolled along the various streets in the Wittenbergplatz and Nollendorfplatz areas, he noticed how the men seemed to look one directly in the eyes. He wasn't sure whether this was a German characteristic or whether they were cruising him, but whatever, he enjoyed their attention.

He wandered down Motzstrasse, passing a number of bars and cafes and came to a café called, Da Neben, and entered. There were a few men and women, sitting drinking coffees and eating breakfasts. There seemed to be a very relaxed atmosphere, with people chatting and laughing. A young waiter came over and Mike ordered a cup of coffee. When the coffee arrived, Mike asked the waiter, " What is the night life like here?"

The young man misunderstood and thought that Mike meant in his café.

"No," replied Mike. "In Berlin!"

"That depends if you go to the old East or stay in the West," said the young man.

"What's the difference? I thought there was no longer a West or East?"

"That is true, but habits don't always change," he said, "In the bars on the old East side, you find people tend to sit and talk, but in the West, there is much more fun, if you know what I mean."

"Oh I do," smiled Mike. "So where do I find these fun places?"

"The most popular place is 'Connection' dance club," said the young man, his face lighting with enthusiasm.

"Why what happens there?" asked Mike.

"Everything!" laughed the young man. "Why don't you just go and find out."

Mike made a mental note of the name and thanked the young man for his advice, drank his coffee, paid and left to continue his tour of this old city.

Mike headed in a Northerly direction, aiming for the famous Tiergarten, which he had heard was a great cruising place. The parklands were beautifully laid out and he wandered through the area, but was surprised to see no action. This disappointed him and he wondered whether Germans were prudes or this whole thing about the Tiergarten being a good cruising area was simply a marketing strategy.

As the day progressed, he wandered up and down many streets and ally-ways looking at the varying architectural structures, both old and new, and admiring the sights of modern and old Berlin. He finally made his way back to his hotel. When he got up to his room, he remembered about Eric having a brother in Berlin, so he thought of telephoning him to see if he could help him to find Barry. He picked up the phone and dialed the number that Eric had given him. It rang and then he heard an answering machine with a message in German. He couldn't understand the German, but he waited until the message was finished and then spoke,

"Hello, my name is Mike and I met your brother Eric in Paris and he told me to phone you. If you'd like to contact me, phone me on 217-8207. Cheers." Then he put down the phone.

Soon after Mike had replaced the telephone, it rang.

"Mike, it's Pierre."

"Hi, Pierre. What news of Barry?"

"I have good news for you my friend. The kidnappers phoned as planned and I did as you suggested and asked them the name of their prisoner. Guess what? You were right. They have taken the wrong person captive. They were devastated when they realized their mistake, and they haven't released Barry; but they're not threatening to kill him any more, however, now they are desperate for the money."

"Did they say where Barry was?" asked Mike.

"No, my friend, unfortunately not, but he is apparently safe."

"Listen Pierre, I've phoned Eric's brother and I hope that he can help me to search around Berlin."

Again Pierre didn't say anything about the possible Czech connection, in the hopes that he might be wrong in thinking that Barry had been moved to the Czech Republic.

"My friend, now that we know that Barry's life is no longer in danger, go out and enjoy yourself. If I hear anything new, I'll contact you and if you're out, I'll leave a message at the hotel," said Pierre.

By 10 p.m. Mike had received no phone call from either Eric's brother or Pierre, so he dressed and went down to the hotel's foyer. There he asked the receptionist where the 'Connection' club was. The receptionist smiled at Mike and said, "Here."

"What do you mean, here?"

"It belongs to the hotel."

Mike laughed embarrassedly. "Well how do I get to it?"

The receptionist explained and Mike headed in the given direction.

When he entered, there must have been between two and three hundred men crammed into the area, dancing to techno music. The mood was festive and light-hearted with everyone obviously out to have a good time. He made his way to the bar and ordered a beer. He stood at the bar watching the dancers and listening to the beat of the music. After a while he leaned across the bar and shouted above the sound of the music to the barman who wore only a pair of cut-off denim shorts.

"I'm new here, but somebody said that things happen here, where?"

The barman shouted back, "upstairs!"

"What's upstairs?"

"The backroom," he shouted back.

This sounded better, Mike thought. "Thanks," he shouted and set off to find his way upstairs.

When he had traveled around and seen what was there, his eyes were ready to pop out of his head. There were two floors of cruising, hundreds of rest cubicles, at least thirty or forty TV sets showing porn and five large rooms, which got progressively darker as you went from one to another. This was heaven, thought Mike, but where does one start?

He went and stood watching one of the porn channels on the TV, but also kept an eye on the passing procession of men. His eye caught a dark-haired youth of about twenty-one, wearing only a pair of Lycra running shorts; his body glistening in the light from the flickering TV screen. The guy saw Mike looking at him and gave a slight nod of his head and moved off towards one of the dark rooms. Mike followed.

The room was large, empty of furniture and was lit by a single candle glowing in a corner. By the time Mike entered the room, he had got his eyes used to the limited light and had seen where the young man was standing; he saw that someone was already feeling the young guy's crotch. As soon as the young guy saw Mike, he pushed the man in front of him away and moved towards Mike. The young man had a rugged look about him. He had dark flashing eyes, high cheekbones and a full mouth. When he got up to Mike, Mike said quietly, "Hi", but the young man never said a word, he merely grabbed Mike's crotch. Mike felt the pain as the man squeezed his balls and he let out an agonizing groan.

Mike reciprocated and did the same to the young man, but the more Mike squeezed, the more the young man smiled. The young man virtually tore Mike's jeans from him as he tried to get access to Mike's dick. Mike was getting harder during all this and the young man could feel it. As he pushed Mike's briefs down, Mike's cock shot upwards. The man's hand squeezed around its shaft and he began to jerk Mike's cock. Using both hands, Mike took hold of the young man's nipples, squeezed them and pulled the nipples towards him. Still there was no reaction from the young man.

The young man went down onto his knees and wrapped his full lips around Mike's long shaft. Mike stood and watched as this hot mouth sank straight down the full ten-inch length of his cock. The young guy looked up at Mike and had that glint in his eyes again as if to say, "How was that? Does that impress you?" He slowly pulled a little way up Mike's cock and ran his tongue around the shaft of his cock. Mike was thoroughly enjoying this pleasurable experience. Mike could also see that the young man's cock was standing erect and that there was a wet spot forming in the front of his Lycra shorts.

Mike put his hands under the young man's arms and lifted him. Once he had the man standing, he gripped the guy's hard cock and rubbed his hand over it. "Hmm, Wet," said Mike, as he went onto his knees and rubbed his lips over the Lycra-covered, wet cock of the young man. The man pulled his shorts down to reveal his throbbing, cut cock waiting to be taken. Mike knelt and looked at its beautiful shape before he wrapped his mouth around it and started slowly sucking up and down its length. As he did so, he looked up and saw the young man smiling at him while he played with his own nipples. The guy started fucking Mike's face, thrusting his cock as far into Mike's mouth as he could get it. Mike looked at the expression on the young man's face and could see that he was enjoying himself. As he pumped into Mike's mouth, Mike could see the man's defined stomach muscles tense and relax. Mike decided to give this young guy his pleasure. He started working over the young guy's cock more roughly using his mouth, tongue and his hand. By this time the young man was sweating profusely and tugging hard at his nipples as though he was about to pull them off. Suddenly he gave one massive push forward and Mike could feel the guy's warm cum start shooting into his mouth. He swallowed and felt the next load already being fired into his throat. He put his hands around the young man's ass and pulled him closer, forcing his dick deeper into Mike's mouth. Mike kept up his movements while the young man's body contorted in spasms as he emptied his load into Mike's throat. The young man began to relax, but Mike never let go, he kept working on his cock. The guy placed his hands at the back of Mike's head and pulled it further onto his dick. Mike ran his tongue around the subsiding cock and sucked, milking every last drop from it. When the young guy's cock was limp, he tried to gain release from Mike's mouth, but Mike just held on, tonguing its length. Mike looked up at the young man, and in the candlelight he saw tears welling up in the guy's eyes. He immediately let go of his cock and stood up. He wrapped his arms around the young man and looked into those wet, glistening eyes.

"What's the matter?" asked Mike.

The young man never said a word, but the tears continued to flow.

"Did I hurt you?"

The young guy simply shook his head. He leaned forward and placed his full lips onto Mike's. Mike opened his mouth to meet the young man's kiss, and the young man's tongue went into the depths of Mike's mouth enabling him to taste the remnants of his own cum. Mike felt the guy's tongue moving around his mouth as though he were trying to clean out Mike's mouth. When their lips parted, the young man spoke for the first time.

"Thank you, that was beautiful. You are so good. My English not good," he stammered.

Mike smiled.

"Your English is good, so are you. What is your name?"

"Gunter."

They stood together, hugging and kissing each other, then they released their hold on each other, pulled up their pants and the young man took Mike by the hand and led him to the bar.

"You are beautiful, and I want to thank you for allowing me to give you such pleasure," said Mike.

Gunter smiled and offered to buy Mike a drink. Mike accepted and the two of them stood at the bar enjoying each other's company.

After spending a wonderful evening together, Mike left the club and went to his room. When he got there, he found a message to say that Eric's brother, Tom, had phoned and that if Mike wanted to see him he would be at a studio the following day from about 11:00 the following morning. He had left the address so Mike thought that as he had nothing planned for the following day, he would try and see Tom.

When he awoke in the morning, he asked for directions to the address that Tom had left for him. He made his way to the address in the hopes that Eric's brother might help him to find Barry. He found it in a rather seedy looking area filled with what looked like disused warehouses. He made his way up to the fourth floor and saw a sign that read, 'Galaxy Studios'. Mike immediately thought back to the video recording they had seen in Pierre's apartment in Paris, where they had seen the letters G-A-L. Was this where the video had been made or was it sheer co-incidence that the first three letters of the studio were the same as those visible in the video? He knocked and entered. There was a young man sitting behind a desk who asked Mike, in German, if he could help him. Mike replied, in English, that he was looking for Tom. The man at the front desk smiled told him that Tom was busy filming in the studio, but that he thought it would be alright if Mike went through to the studio. The young man lustfully eyed Mike as he departed the reception area.

Mike went down a passageway and entered a large, sparsely furnished room. As he entered he saw that a film crew were busy filming. In the center of the room was a set depicting a bedroom, and adjacent to it was another set depicting a kitchen.

The bedroom set contained a bed and nothing else, while the kitchen set had a counter, a table and some chairs. There were about six people in the studio and lights and cables were scattered everywhere. He looked towards the bedroom set and saw two guys lying on the bed together. The set looked familiar. It had all the bearings of the bedroom set in the video. This was becoming eerie to Mike.

Someone, obviously the director, was shouting instructions in German and every time he did so, the two on the bed changed their positions, while cameras also changed theirs. Mike moved a little closer so that he could see what was happening on the bed and take in the rest of the room. One of the guys on the bed was sitting on the cock of the other, while a camera was positioned between the legs of the guy whose cock was being ridden. Mike had never seen a porn film being made; come to think of it, he had never seen any film being made. He felt an arousal between his legs as he watched the two guys. As he watched, he wondered if the cameramen and the director also felt aroused by the scene in front of them.

He moved in closer and as he did so, he accidentally bumped into one of the light stands. The crew immediately turned to see what had caused this and saw Mike. The director shouted something in German and Mike just shrugged his shoulders and said, "I'm sorry, I didn't mean to disturb."

"What do you want?" shouted the director, abruptly.

"I was looking for Tom," said Mike rather sheepishly.

The guy who was sitting on the other guy's cock turned and said, "I am Tom."

"Hi, I'm Mike. I phoned you and you phoned me back." Mike could see that Tom was a little embarrassed by the situation. He climbed off the guy's cock and walked naked to Mike with his own cock swaying in front as he did so, and shook hands with him. Mike could see that Tom was just as well blessed in size as Eric was.

"Take a seat," said Tom, "this could take some time, so sit and relax."

The director then snapped an order in English. "Take five everybody," and the crew stopped doing their work and sat to relax.

"I'm sorry if I got you into trouble," said Mike, as Tom returned to him, "but I've never been in a film studio."

"Oh it's all right," said Tom. "Don't worry about the director, he's always like this."

Mike then leaned close to Tom and said, "Can I ask you a personal question?"

"Sure," came the reply.

"How do you keep a hard-on when you're filming. I mean with these other people around you and with all the stopping and starting?"

Tom laughed, " You get used to it. Sometimes it's very difficult, but if the guy you're working with is sexy, then you have no problems."

Just then the director called everyone to their positions.

"Right, Kurt, get on that bed but this time open your legs wider so that the camera can get in between them. Tom get onto his dick and we'll take it from where you lie forward so that we can see his full length going up you."

The two guys got onto the bed, but Kurt's dick had become soft during the break.

"Tom! Get his dick hard again," shouted the director.

Tom immediately put his mouth to Kurt's dick and started to suck him, eventually getting it hard again. When Kurt was once again erect, Tom slipped onto it.

"Action!" shouted the direction.

Tom leant his body forward and Mike could see Kurt's dick deeply embedded in Tom's ass.

"Right, ride that cock," shouted the director, and Tom started to rise and fall onto Kurt's dick.

This continued for a while until the director shouted, "Cut!" And the two guys stopped their action. Tom remained impaled on Kurt's dick while they waited for the director's instructions.

"Where is Manfred?" shouted the director.

There was silence.

When there was no reply, the director screamed loudly, "Where is Manfred? Will somebody tell me?"

The young man who had been at the front desk when Mike had arrived at the studio scuttled in to see what all the noise was about.

When the director saw him he yelled, "Where is Manfred?"

"I don't know. He didn't phone to say that he wasn't coming in," replied the young man.

"He is supposed to be part of this scene and because he's not here, we can't film the sequence."

Tom looked across at Mike.

"What about him?" asked Tom, pointing to Mike.

The director looked at Mike and said, "Take off your clothes."

Mike was so surprised by the tone of the order that he immediately obeyed.

He pulled his shirt off to reveal his well-built physique, then he dropped is jeans. As he stood there in the G-string that Pierre had bought him, everyone's mouths dropped open as they saw the bulge that was hidden in the G-string's pouch.

The director stared at the bulge and moved slowly towards Mike. He pointed at Mike's G-string and said, "Is that thing stuffed with anything?"

Mike looked down at his bulge, looked back at the director and said, "Yes, my cock!"

The director let out a gasp and said, "Take that thing off."

Mike latched his thumbs into the sides of the G-string, turned his back on his audience, pushed his G-string down and then bent to step out of it. There were gasps from everyone when they saw his beautifully firm ass, but there were even greater gasps when Mike eventually turned to face his audience. His dick had swollen and was standing straight out ahead of him.

When the director saw this majestic sight, his mind rushed and he shouted, "We re-film."

"What!" exclaimed one of the cameramen.

"We change," shouted the director. "Kurt, I want you to play Manfred's part and you – what is your name?"

"Mike."

" …you will play Kurt's part."

Kurt looked a little upset at losing his part and the director could see this.

"Kurt, his dick is much bigger and thicker than yours and that's the sort of thing our viewers want. You must make your entry when Tom is riding his dick and go to Tom's head so that he can take your dick into his mouth and start sucking you. Right places everybody."

Mike moved over to the bed and lay down. Tom rose over him and said, "I think I'm going to enjoy this, and I don't think I'll lose my hard-on."

He slipped his ass gently onto Mike's huge bargepole, screwing his face in agony as its thickness stretched his ass muscles.

"Ready," shouted the director.

"Not yet," came Tom's reply. "This guy is the biggest I've ever had and I need to get used to it."

"Well be quick," snapped the director.

Tom began to rise and fall on Mike's dick and Mike could see that he was enjoying it. While Tom was "getting used to it", the others were chatting quietly.

"Are you sure you aren't used to it yet?" asked Mike, smiling at Tom.

"I think I need a bit more time," replied Tom, who was thriving on this pleasure.

"Rubbish! Action," shouted the director.

Tom continued his rhythmic movement on Mike's cock.

"Right, Tom, lean forward onto his stomach and chest."

Tom did as he was told and the camera moved for a close up shot of the base of Mike's cock disappearing into Tom's smooth ass.

"Thrust upwards. Make Tom rise into the air," shouted the director to Mike. Mike did as he was told and Tom continued to ride him. Their mouths were now attached and when the director saw this he shouted, "Camera two, get onto the kiss. Camera one, stay on his dick. Tom, I want you to lift your ass higher so that we can see the full length of Mike's cock. That's better. Camera one, move in closer. Good."

This continued for a while and then the director shouted, "Cut," but Tom and Mike were too involved in their passion.

"Cut!" shouted the director again. This time Tom's mouth parted from Mike's and he looked at the director.

"I said, Cut, and when I say that I mean, Cut," reprimanded the director.

He moved up to the bed and said, "Tom, I want you to wrap your legs around Mike. If you have to roll over onto your side to do it, then that's fine."

Tom rose off Mike's cock. "Stay on," shouted the director.

Tom didn't need a second invitation, so he sank back onto Mike's cock. He tried to wrap his legs around Mike, but found it difficult, so Mike moved over onto his side, which allowed Tom to do as the director had instructed.

"Right, cameras ready. Action!"

Mike began thrusting into Tom as he held tightly onto him. Tom's legs, in the meantime, were clamped around Mike's waist thus forcing Mike's cock deeper into him.

"Mike, roll him onto his back so that you are then on top."

Mike did as he was told, but still Tom never let go and still forced himself deeper onto Mike's cock.

"Right, Mike, lift his legs into the air. That's it. Now pull right back so that we can just see the tip of your dick, but don't let it slip out."

Mike again did as he was told. When it felt as if he was about to slip out, the director shouted, "Now ram it in. Good! Do it again and keep doing this. Camera one get right up next to that shaft and follow its entry. Camera two get above Tom's chest and focus a shot down towards Tom's dick so that we can get another view of this penetration. The cameras moved into their allotted positions.

This action continued for some time and then the director shouted, "Kurt I want you to come in and move up to Tom's face for the blow-job sequence. Come into camera view, Kurt."

Kurt, who had been watching the action and who had got very hard, had pre-cum oozing from the tip of his dick. The director saw this and shouted to Kurt, "Don't wipe that pre-cum from your dick, I like it. Move over to Tom and I want him to lick it off you, then I want you to squeeze your dick and see if you can milk any more from it."

Kurt walked to where Tom's head was and pushed the stem of his dick towards Tom's mouth. Tom's tongue shot out and licked the pre-cum from the tip. Tom licked his lips and Kurt tightened the grip around the base of his dick and squeezed some more pre-cum out of the opening at the tip. Again Tom's tongue did the work, but this time, instead of just licking it, he engulfed Kurt's dick and started sucking. Camera two focused on Kurt's dick sliding in and out of Tom's mouth, while camera one was busy at the other end of Tom, watching Mike's penetration.

Throughout this action, Mike noticed that the director had been feeling his own erection in his pants.

"Cut!" shouted the director.

Kurt pulled his dick from Tom's mouth and Mike let his slide out of Tom's ass. The three men waited for their next instructions.

"Are you guys getting close?" enquired the director.

Tom said that he was, but Mike and Kurt were still some way from coming.

"OK," said the director, "I want you to go back to your previous positions, but now Kurt I want you to let Tom suck you, but you must lean across his chest and also suck him. Tom, when you are ready to come, tell us, and Kurt you must move off his dick so that the camera can catch him shooting. Mike you just carry on fucking him."

"Right, Action!"

The men went back to their action and it wasn't very long after that Tom said that he was going to shoot. Kurt removed his mouth from Tom's dick and Tom began jerking his own dick. The first of his white cum shot up onto his chest, soon to be followed by a flood of more. Tom continued to gobble on Kurt's hard muscle as he shot his load. Mike could feel Tom's ass muscles clamp around his cock and for a moment, the feeling was so great that he thought he was going to come, but he managed to hold it off. When Tom had finished coming, the director shouted, "Cut!"

"Right Tom, go and clean yourself up and you two, move over to the kitchen set. Mike pulled out of Tom and sauntered over to the new set. Kurt followed.

"Now what?" asked Mike.

"I'm not sure what he's got in mind," said Kurt, but I think the idea is that this is where you fuck me."

Tom returned to where the filming was taking place, having cleaned himself up.

"OK guys, let's get some action again. Kurt I want you to sit on the edge of the kitchen table and Mike, I want you to go between his legs and suck his dick. When I tell you, I want you to push Kurt onto his back, pull his ass to the edge of the table if necessary, lift his legs into the air and then fuck him. Is that clear?"

They said that they fully understood.

"Do you want me to be hard when we start the shot?" asked Kurt.

"No, we'll start with you already on the table and with Mike's mouth around your dick. Places everybody. Action!"

The cameras started rolling and so did Mike's actions. One cameraman lay under the edge of the table and looked up, while the other waited for instructions.

After a while, the director told Mike to pull Kurt to the edge of the table and to lift his legs. Mike rose to a standing position and pulled Kurt's body towards the edge of the table. He positioned himself close to Kurt's ass and aimed his now erect dick at the entry. The camera that was under the edge of the table was busy filming the entry, while the other camera now showed the view from the side.

Mike plunged into Kurt's ass and started his rhythmic fuck. As he did so, the director watched Mike's stomach and ass muscles tighten and then relax.

"Camera two, focus onto Mike's ass I want to see it clench and relax as he fucks Kurt. Camera one, come up and shoot a high angled shot so we get Mike's stomach muscles as well as his cock sliding in and out."

The cameramen followed instructions.

"Tom," shouted the director, "I want you to enter the scene and kneel behind Mike's ass and start licking it. Pull his ass cheeks apart and lick his hole."

Tom moved into the picture and knelt behind Mike. Mike could feel Tom's warm breath on his ass and it felt great. Tom pulled Mike's muscular ass cheeks apart and stared at the small pink opening that confronted him. He moved his tongue in and wet the opening. Mike ground deeper into Kurt when Tom did this. Tom's tongue worked feverishly.

"Camera two, focus on Tom rimming him."

Tom pulled Mike's cheeks as far apart as they would go and spat some saliva onto Mike's opening. Tom rubbed a finger over the opening, spreading his saliva. He spat again and did the same, but this time he gently began to insert a finger. As he did so, he felt Mike push back onto his finger, causing it to sink into Mike's ass. Tom's finger went in and out. He removed his finger and spat again. This time he inserted two fingers. Mike groaned in ecstasy as Tom's young fingers worked their way around the inside of Mike's ass. The director hadn't planned this, but he could see that both men were enjoying it.

"Tom, I want you to loosen Mike's ass up and then I want you to slip your dick into that pink eye that you're looking at," said the director, who at this stage was so engrossed by the action that he had taken his own dick from his pants and was jerking himself off.

Tom spat again, rubbing it over and in the opening. This time he inserted three fingers and the camera could see Mike's asshole spreading open like a fish getting ready to swallow some food. Tom stood up but kept his fingers firmly place in Mike's ass. Mike, in the meantime was sweating profusely as he rammed his cock deeper into Kurt.

He turned his head towards Tom and in a breathy tone said, "Take me Tom. Come, kid, fuck this ass. I want that cock of yours pounding in my hot ass."

Tom positioned his cock at Mike's asshole and slowly started to push forward. When Mike felt this, he couldn't wait for Tom's slow entry, and he pushed back impaling himself on Tom's entire length. Tom gasped as he felt his cock suddenly immersed in Mike's tight ass. Once Tom was inside him, Mike bucked like a mad animal, pounding his own throbbing cock deep into Kurt and thrusting his tight ass deeply onto Tom's cock.

"Fuck my ass," shouted Mike. "Push that cock in. Deeper! Fuck me baby!"

Tom was battling to keep himself steady as he held on to Mike's strong hips. The kitchen table was creaking and Kurt was being thrust backwards and forwards on the table. The amount of sexual energy that was being exuded in the kitchen scene was phenomenal. The two cameramen were moving all over the place. They didn't need directions because they just knew where to be, and also because the director had his pants down around his ankles and was too busy breathing heavily as he jerked his dick to give them directions. Kurt was groaning on the table, his breathing coming steadily quicker.

"I'm going to come," bellowed Kurt. A cameraman leapt in to shoot the moment of Kurt's eruption.

"Aaargh!" cried Kurt as he shot his load over his chest and onto the lens of the camera.

The cameraman shouted to his buddy, "I've got cum on my lens, take over." Quickly he wiped his lens and prepared to continue filming.

As Kurt shot, his sphincter squeezed around Mike's cock. Mike realized that he couldn't hold on any longer; the tightness he was experiencing was too great for him to contain himself.

"Tom, I coming," shouted Mike, gasping as his climax grew ever nearer.

Tom let go of Mike's hips and placed both hands on Mike's nipples and twisted them.

"Aaaargh, Fuuuck!" screamed Mike. "Fuck my ass, kid. Deeper! Harder! Fuck me baby."

Mike ground his ass against Tom's stomach and felt Tom's cock jerk in a spasm as the warm feeling of Tom's cum entered his bowels. Both men pushed against each other as they shot their loads. The room reverberated with the sound of gasping, moaning, swearing and intense heavy breathing as each person fulfilled his desires. When they were emptied, Tom rested his head on Mike's shoulders and Mike leaned forward across Kurt's stomach. There was silence and then they heard applause. They raised their tired heads and saw the director standing watching them, applauding. At the foot of the director, on the floor, lay a puddle of liquid where he had shot, and when they looked at the cameramen, both had a hard-on and a wet patch in the front of their pants.

"Cut," said a tired, feeble voice, "that's a wrap!"

Once they had cleaned themselves, Mike said that he wanted to speak privately to Tom, but chose not to elaborate on why.

Mike and Tom headed back to Mike's hotel after they had cleaned up, dressed and the filming was finished, and on the way, Tom said, "the director wants to know whether you would like to make a few more films for him?"

Mike roared with laughter, "I'm no actor."

"It's not about acting," said Tom, "it's about sex appeal and the size of your cock, and I think you qualify on both counts."

"Do you do this on a full-time basis, Tom?" asked Mike.

"Do you mean making porno films?"

"Your brother said you were a model."

"Sure I do modeling, but I make more money as a stripper and a porno star."

"You're also a stripper!" exclaimed Mike.

"Well, if you've got the goods, flaunt them, and I don't know why you don't, because you've certainly got the goods."

"I don't know if I could do it," said Mike.

"Well you did it today, and I believe you did it in Paris." Tom gave a wry smile when he said that.

"Has Eric been speaking to you?"

"He phoned me early this morning to ask whether you had contacted me and he told me about the competition. He also told me what a hunk and a good fuck you were, and he's right."

"But if I'm a good fuck, you owe me one," said Mike.

"What do you mean I owe you one?"

"You've fucked my ass and shot your load into me, but you haven't had a taste of my hot cum," said Mike, winking at Tom.

"Well I'm sure there'll be an opportunity for you," said Tom, squeezing Mike cock.

"What are you doing tonight?" asked Mike.

"Why, what did you have in mind?"

"I thought maybe we could get together," said Mike sounding

hopeful.

"Well, I'm not sure," said Tom, sounding as though he was playing hard to get.

"That's the problem with you young hunks, once you've had an older man, you want to dump them," said Mike sounding sorry for himself.

"You're doing this on purpose," said Tom, "trying to make me feel guilty."

"Well are you?"

"You don't give up do you?"

"Not when I have a nice young hunk around me," laughed Mike. "So what about tonight?"

"I'm doing a show tonight, but would *you* like to come and see it?"

"Sure, "said Mike, "where?"

"At a club called 'CC96' from 8p.m."

"What sort of show is it?" asked Mike.

"Come and see, and maybe you'll get what I owe you."

"But Tom, I need to speak to you about something more important than you and me."

"What could be that important?" enquired Tom.

"Come up to my room because I need to speak privately."

"Are you sure it's to speak?" teased Tom, with a glint in his eye.

"Yes, it is; seriously."

When they arrived at Mike's room, they went in and Mike locked the bedroom door.

"This looks serious, you locking the door," said Tom.

"It's just that I don't want anyone coming in while we're talking."

Tom sat on the edge of the bed while Mike stood facing him.

"Tom, is your studio used for anything other than making porno movies?"

"I don't understand what you mean, Mike?"

"Tom, I have to trust you with what I'm about to tell you."

"Of course you can," replied the young man.

"While I was in Paris, your brother, a friend of ours and myself went out one night. When we returned we found out that my nephew, who was traveling with me, had been kidnapped."

"Oh yes, Eric did say something about trouble in Paris, but he didn't elaborate."

"Well, the kidnappers threatened to kill my nephew if the ransom money wasn't paid up. However, that apparently has changed because I've since found out that they've realized that they have the wrong guy. Why I asked you about the studio is because we received a video of my nephew being raped on a bed in a room …"

"…that's heavy."

"But when we looked carefully at the background of the room," continued Mike, "we saw the letters G-A-L. The rest of the letters were blocked by his legs being in the way. I became suspicious when I visited you today because where you're filming is Galaxy Studios, and the first three letters are the same as were in the video."

Tom looked horrified.

"Do you think they might have held him in the studio?" asked Tom.

"That I don't know, but when I first came into the studio and saw the set on which you were performing, the bedroom scene looked exactly the same as in the video."

Tom's mind raced as he tried to think who might be involved in the kidnapping, if it had in fact been filmed in the studio.

"Mike, this comes as a total surprise to me. I can't think who might do anything like that. But tell me, were there any other distinguishing features in the video that might help us to determine if it was filmed here?"

Mike thought for a while, and then replied: "There was a calendar and it had the word Berlin on it, and that's why I headed here."

"What about the man you saw raping your nephew? Did you see his face or were there any distinguishing marks or features that you might have noticed?"

Again Mike thought hard.

"The only thing I can say was that the guy who was fucking Barry, that's my nephew, was uncut and had a long, thick cock, but then that could be quite common here."

"If you say he was fucking your nephew, how do you know he was uncut?" enquired Tom.

"We caught a glimpse of him at the foot of the bed before he penetrated Barry."

Tom thought for a moment and then said, "Being uncut is not that common. You see of all of those working in the studio that I know of, there's only one guy who is uncut and has a big cock."

"Who's that?" asked Mike.

"Kurt. Everybody else has a cut cock."

"Do you think it could be him?"

"I wouldn't know," answered Tom.

"What do you know about Kurt?" asked Mike, sitting down on the bed next to Tom.

"I know that he's not German and he only recently arrived on the set. Where he was working before coming here I'm not sure, but I did hear that he'd made some porno movies in Prague."

"That's in the Czech Republic, isn't it?"

"Yes, but other than that, I can't tell you much."

"Tom, do you think that somehow we might be able to talk to him tomorrow, alone?"

"I don't see why not. We have got a scene to shoot and he's in it, so maybe if you come to the studio, we can chat to him."

Although Mike was relieved to know that Barry's life was no longer in danger, he was still concerned about his safety, especially as he'd seen how drugged Barry had looked in the video.

"Well, I suppose there's nothing much I can do at the moment until we speak to Kurt," murmured Mike, still thinking about Barry.

"I told you to come to the club and see the show tonight and that might take your mind off things," said Tom, offering some support to Mike.

That evening, Mike showered and pulled on his leather jeans and a T-shirt and made his way to the 'CC96' club, not knowing what to expect. Mike went in and headed for the bar, once he had got his bearings inside the club. At the counter were a number of young men, naked from the waist up. They were very friendly and welcomed Mike to the club.

"Is this your first visit?" asked a boy who looked no more than eighteen-years-old and had a young smooth body.

"Yes," replied Mike.

The boy ran his hand over Mike's shoulders. 'If there is anything you would like, please don't hesitate to ask," he said coyly.

Mike looked around the club but couldn't see Tom anywhere. Music was playing loudly and a number of male topless dancers were dancing on the bar counter, wrapping themselves suggestively around poles and a couple were dancing in cages. At the bar counter, Mike bought some of the club's 'CC96-cent-notes' to slip to any of the dancers who he might think is sexy or attractive. The guys who were dancing were older than twenty and obviously all worked out at a gym, because they had beautifully defined bodies. Some of the dancers wore denim jeans, all tightly fitting, showing off their cute butts or their bulges, while others had cut-off denim shorts.

A pretty well-built guy with a well-tanned body, in a pair of jeans, came and started dancing on the bar counter in front of Mike. Mike sat there, mesmerized by the sight. He swiveled his ass in front of Mike and he could see what a tight ass this guy had. Then the dancer turned to face Mike and rubbed his hand over his crotch. He crouched in front of Mike and thrust his pelvis towards him. Mike liked what he saw so he took some of his 'CC' money and slipped it into the front of the dancer's jeans, smiling at the guy as he did so. There were now a few more dancers and Mike didn't know who to look at as they maneuvered themselves around the bar counter. Once again, the eighteen-year old boy came back to Mike.

"Are you enjoying yourself?"

"Yes thank you," said Mike politely.

"Would you like to buy me a drink?" asked the boy.

Mike didn't want to be rude, but he wasn't attracted to this young boy. "I'm actually waiting for a friend," said Mike, trying to avoid answering the question.

The boy didn't give up.

"I can sit here with you until he comes."

"Well, actually I think he's here already," said Mike.

"Oh, I don't see any one with you. Where is he?"

"He's doing a show here tonight," said Mike, who was now getting irritated by the boy.

When the boy heard this, he simply gave Mike a rather indignant look, and walked off.

Yet another dancer moved along the bar counter and stopped in front of Mike. He was a tall, dark-haired guy with a huge chest, slim waist and a washboard stomach. He too was wearing tight blue jeans with the white top of his briefs sticking above his jeans waistband. This to Mike was a very sexy sight, as he began to imagine what might be hidden in those white briefs. The young man stood with his legs wide apart above Mike. Mike looked up at the man and smiled at him. The young man slid both his hands down over his stomach muscles until both his thumbs hooked into the waistband of his jeans. He continued to pull down and so force the waistband lower and with his other fingers, wrapped them around the huge pack in his jeans and squeezed. Mike stared at this bulge and thought of his own. His hands automatically went to his own crotch and he squeezed his erect cock. The young man saw this and saw the size of the bulge in Mike's jeans. The dancer swiveled his hips and thrust his crotch forward. Mike squeezed his cock again and then rubbed his hand over its length, outlining its shape and size for the dancer. The dancer knelt in front of Mike, still thrusting his hips forward towards him, and then he slowly unzipped his jeans, their eyes penetrating each other. Mike could see the white bikini briefs under the guy's jeans. The dancer slid his hand into the fly of his jeans and rubbed his hand over his swelling bulge. Mike leaned forward with some of his 'CC' money, rubbed his hand over the bulge, felt that the young guy was quite hard, and then slipped the money down into the front of his briefs. As he did so, his hand touched the head of the dancer's dick, which throbbed as he did so. The dancer never moved away after he had received the money, but rather continued to gyrate in front of Mike until he was lying on his back on the bar counter. His face was towards Mike's and Mike watched as the guy thrust his hips into the air in a fucking motion and then relaxed back on the counter. He repeated this motion a number of times causing Mike's cock to get harder every time the guy did it.

The dancer then rolled over onto his stomach and began to raise and lower his ass on the counter, as though he was fucking the counter. He let his hand droop over the edge of the counter near Mike's crotch. As he continued to 'fuck' the counter, his hand moved to Mike's jeans and wrapped his hand around the length of Mike's hard cock. For the first time he spoke, "that feels good and so big!" He gave Mike's cock another squeeze and then rolled onto his back again. As he did so, Mike caught a glimpse of the dancer's bulge and saw a wet stain on his white briefs. Once again he thrust his hips skyward. Mike stood up so that he was now looking down on the dancer lying on the counter, gave him a broad grin and put his hand on the dancer's bulge. As he did so he felt the wetness of his briefs. He then took the waistband of his briefs, pulled it down to reveal the guy's cut cock, kissed it and slipped another piece of money into his briefs, then covered the guy's cock with his briefs, gave the bulge another kiss and sat down again.

While the dancer was still on his back, he lifted his hips into the air, zipped up his jeans and rose to his feet again, adjusting the swollen bulge as he did so. He winked at Mike and danced off. Mike could feel that his own cock had been dribbling in his briefs and he felt his own wetness.

After a while all the dancers left their dance platforms and an announcer came forward.

"Gentlemen, could I have your attention. The CC 96 Club is proud to present yet another talented young stripper for your pleasure. Please welcome Tom."

Mike swung round to face the dance floor. The lights faded and a spotlight shone onto the center of the dance area. The volume of the music rose and into the spotlight came Tom. Everyone applauded and whistled their approval. Mike watched as Tom gyrated his slim hips and started unbuttoning his shirt in time to the music. He moved well, thought Mike. People began to crowd around the dance floor, forming a circle, which meant that Mike's view was now being obstructed so he stood up to watch.

Tom's shirt came off and he tantalizingly wrapped it around a customer's neck and the customer ran his fingers over Tom's smooth chest, making sure that he touched the two protruding nipples. Tom then moved around the circle to someone else, thrusting his pelvis at the man.

While Mike was standing watching the strip show, he felt a hard bulge touch his butt. He never looked around, nor did he move. The hardness of the bulge pushed a little harder onto his butt. That felt firm and big thought Mike. There were a number of people standing close by and Mike slowly turned his head to see whose bulge it was. As he turned, he saw it was the dancer who had touched him up earlier. Their eyes met once more and it was as if a bond was created between them. When he knew who it was, Mike pushed back onto the dancer's bulging pack. The dancer put his arms around Mike and stood there with his hands clasping Mike's crotch. Every now and then, the dancer would give a thrust forward and Mike would thrust back.

By this time, Tom had removed the jeans that he was wearing and was now moving through the crowd in a G-string. People were slipping 'CC' money into the back, sides and front of his G-string. He suddenly caught sight of Mike and started to move towards him. The crowd parted to allow Tom to move through until he came face-to-face with Mike. Mike at this stage was still standing with the dancer behind him, but he had put his arms behind the dancer's back and onto his ass and was pulling the dancer closer to him. Tom dance seductively in front of Mike and could see the other dancer's hands grasping onto Mike's now fully erect cock. Tom rubbed his crotch against the other dancer's hands. The dancer smiled and gently squeezed Tom's dick, but Tom wasn't satisfied, so he pulled the dancers hands away, bent down quickly and kissed Mike's hard-on. He then turned around and danced back in to the middle of the circle. The dancer's hands immediately went back to holding Mike's cock. The climax of the strip was nearing and Tom took hold of the sides of his G-string and in a flash, he stood there naked with his thick cock bouncing up and down, hitting his stomach as he did so.

The audience cheered their approval and money was thrown onto the floor while one of the staff members ran around collecting it. Tom bowed, blew a kiss to the audience and disappeared to his changing room. The lights came up and Mike turned to face his dancer. The dancer kept his arms wrapped around Mike.

"And whom do we have here?" said the dancer.

"Hi, my name's Mike, and whose big bulge am I pressing up against?" asked Mike with a cheeky smile.

"This big bulge as you call it, belongs to Steven."

"Hi, Steven, would you like a drink?" asked Mike, staring deeply into the soft blue eyes that returned the stare.

"Thanks, Mike, a beer please."

Mike ordered the drinks and the two men stood smiling at each other, not knowing what to say to each other at first. They looked deeply into each other's eyes, as though searching for an inner soul.

"I must give you a compliment," said Mike, "I think you danced beautifully in front of me."

"Thank you," said Steven. "Are you here with anybody?"

"I never actually came with anybody, but Tom the stripper asked me to come and see the show, so I suppose you could say I'm here with him."

"Does that mean that you're going home with him?" asked Steven.

"No, not at all," replied Mike, "I choose who I go home with."

Just then, Tom came over to join them.

"Well what did you think of the show?"

Both men complimented Tom and said how they had enjoyed his strip show and how much they thought the audience had also enjoyed it.

"Are you working late tonight, Steven?" asked Tom.

"No, I did a late shift last night, so I'm free tonight," replied Steven.

"Do you mean we don't have to pay for you?" joked Mike.

"Well if *you* want me for the night, it's free, but if one of the other customers wants me, they'll have to pay for it," said Steven.

"And he's not cheap," chirped Tom. "So what's happening tonight?"

Mike looked a little awkward because Tom had invited him out and he had said that Tom still owed him, but now Steven had appeared on the scene, and he really liked the look of Steven. Obviously he could go home on his own, but how could he refuse two good-looking, sexy guys. Steven could sense that something was worrying Mike.

"Are you trying to choose between us, by any chance?" asked Steven.

"Are you psychic?" asked Mike, laughing nervously.

"If you want to go with Tom, I'll understand."

"Listen," said Tom, "I've got a suggestion. I want to go home and have a shower, so why don't you both come back to my place?"

"That's OK by me," said Mike. "How about you Steven?"

"I like the idea. Shall we go if we're not going to do anything else here?"

The three of them called a cab and set off for Tom's apartment.

Tom's apartment was quite an eye-opener. The lounge and kitchen were very ordinary, but his bedroom was interesting because situated on the ceiling above the double bed was a huge mirror, obviously for those moments when one has nothing else to do but look at oneself.. The second bedroom was relatively empty. Tom had placed a masseur's massage table in the center of the room and around the walls were a variety of gym weights and a bench press.

"So this is where you build up that young body of yours," said Steven.

"If I don't feel like going to the gym, then I just stay home and exercise," replied Tom. "But listen guys, make yourselves at home, I just want to have a shower. Of course you're welcome to join me if you'd like."

"Thanks," echoed the other two.

Tom went off to the shower while Mike and Steven picked up a couple of weights and started flexing their muscles. Mike then went and sat on the massage table and watched Steven picking up weights.

"Why don't you strip when you do that?" asked Mike.

Steven smiled at Mike and said, "Would you like that?"

"Very much so," replied Mike.

"Only on condition, my audience also strips," said Steven.

Mike laughed, got off the table and stripped off his clothes. Steven took off his shirt and rubbed his hands over his chest as he watched Mike peel off his clothes. When Mike got to his briefs, Steven said, "Stop! Don't take them off yet."

Steven took off his jeans and stood facing Mike in his white bikini briefs. He moved towards Mike and pressed his crotch against Mike's. They put their arms around each other and stood there letting their cocks grow harder inside their briefs. Eventually, Mike couldn't contain himself any more and started to pull Steven's down and Steven did the same to Mike until they both stood there naked, admiring each other's body.

Steven moved over to the bench press and lay on his back. He picked up two bar bells and slowly began to lift them up and down, flexing his arms as he used them. Mike stood by, watching as Steven's arm and stomach muscles flexed. Steven put them on the floor and said to Mike, "Put some weights onto this bar and help me with some weight exercises."

Mike moved over to the weights lying on the floor and picked up two

25- kilogram weights and placed them on one end of the bar. He then repeated the procedure on the other side of the bar.

"Stand over me and help me in case I drop them," said Steven.

Mike went and stood behind Steven's head and waited for him to pick up the bar.

Steven stared at Mike's erect dick and big balls, which hung over his head. A smile started to form on Steven's face.

"What are you grinning at?" asked Mike.

"I was just wondering if I picked these weights up whether I could rest them on that big cock of yours."

Mike laughed and threatened to beat him up if he tried. Mike helped Steven pick up the bar and watched as he did a few lifts and then put the bar back in its resting place. Each time Steven did a lift, Mike's cock throbbed, as though he might have been visualizing Steven picking him up much like he was doing to the bar, and thrusting his large German cock into Mike.

"Come on Mike, you give it a try."

Steven got off the bench and Mike lay down on it. Steven went to behind Mike's head and helped him lift the bar. Mike pushed it up and down a few times and as he was doing this, Steven moved to in front of Mike.

"Where are you going?" said Mike panting as he exerted the weight.

"Don't worry, I'm here for you," said Steven who had straddled Mikes chest. Steven's cock was now hanging right near Mike's mouth and Mike could see this.

"I can't concentrate," gasped Mike, letting the bar drop, but before it could hit him, Steven caught it and placed it back in its rack. Once he had done that, he remained astride Mike's chest. Mike lifted his head so that he could reach Steven's cock. He pulled Steven's shaft closer to his mouth and licked the tip of it and kissed it.

"That's quite a length," said Mike.

"Nine and a half inches," said Steven.

"I Like someone my own size," said Mike with a glint in his eyes.

"Well would you like this?" asked Steven.

Mike licked his lips and kissed it again.

They hadn't heard Tom come into the room after his shower. He stood in the doorway; his body still wet from his shower and his cock in his hand as he silently jerked himself and watched his two friends.

"Do you want my ass?" asked Mike.

"I want that tight ass more than anything else," said Steven, dangling his cock over Mike's nose and mouth. He moved slightly further up Mike's chest so that his cock could slide easily into Mike's mouth. As he did so, Tom moved silently into the room behind Steven. Because Steven had such a hard-on, he had to bend slightly so that his cock could get into Mike's mouth. In bending, his butt was revealed to Tom whose tongue came out to wet the pink opening. As he touched Steven, Steven jumped.

"Hell, you gave me a fright," said Steven as he climbed off Mike.

"Don't let me stop you Steven," said Tom.

Mike was still lying on the bench. Tom went over to Mike's dick and placed his warm mouth over it, letting his tongue revolve around its shaft. Steven watched this. He moved back to Mike and lowered his dick towards Mike's mouth. Mike swallowed Steven's thick dick into the depths of his throat and sucked. After some time, Tom stood up and said, "Why don't we get on the massage bed?"

Steven helped Mike to his feet and led him to the bed. He gently pushed Mike onto the bed so that he was on his back and his legs were dangling over the edge.

Steven lifted Mike's legs so that his feet were resting on the edge of the bed. Steven then went down to Mike's cock and balls and saturated them with his saliva, kissing and licking them. Tom in the meantime had taken his young cock to Mike's mouth where it was being re-washed with all the sucking and licking that Mike was giving him.

Tom said to Mike, "Remember, I owe you one."

Mike released Tom's dick and said, "Well, then ride this stallion, kid."

Tom moved to the side of the bed and climbed on, astride Mike's cock.

Steven watched as Tom engulfed Mike's cock.

Steven raised Mike's legs causing Tom to move slightly forward on Mike's cock. Once he had got Mike's legs in the air, he positioned his thick nine and a half inch cock at Mike's entrance and pushed. Mike gasped and his sphincter clenched around Steven's rock-hard cock.

Steven froze for a moment as did Tom, then the action started, slowly at first until their passion took over. Tom bounced on Mike's cock as though he were riding a horse while Steven was pile-driving his way into the inner depths of Mike's tight ass. All three men were groaning in ecstasy as they took their pleasure with each other. Tom leaned forward to kiss Mike's mouth and the movement opened his ass wider for Mike. Mike heaved upwards when he felt this opening and Tom gasped as he felt his prostate being massaged by the head of Mike's cock. He knew he wasn't going to last much longer with this action. He released his mouth from Mike's and let out a cry and increased his ferocious riding of Mike's cock. He threw his head back, howled and let forth a flow of cum that poured from his throbbing young cock The first shot hit Mike's chin and the ones that followed covered his chest and stomach. His sphincter was clamping tightly onto Mike's thick cock, not letting go, almost strangling Mike's shaft. Mike could feel the pressure that Tom was exerting on his cock. He could feel it swelling, getting ready to shoot. His body shook and he rammed up into Tom's ass, just as Steven rammed into his. Both men were coming at the same time. Their gasps, moans and shouts were enough to wake the dead.

"Fuck!" growled Steven, as he pumped into Mike, almost pushing him off the bed.

"Fuck me! Oh yes! Oh fuck!" cried Mike as he met each thrust from Steven and pounded into Tom.

Their sweating and heaving bodies thrashed against one another as they fired load after load. Arms, mouths and hands were everywhere as the explosion erupted.

The three men eventually collapsed in a heap on the bed, Tom covering Mike's chest and so rubbing his cum over his own chest, and Steven resting across the back of Tom, but still well embedded in Mike's ass; their breathing was heavy and labored, but soon it began to revert to deep sighs as each man came off his plateau and back to normality.

After they had disentangled themselves, the three of them went through to Tom's bedroom and collapsed onto the double bed, exhausted, but that still didn't stop them during the night. Tom was the perfect host and saw to it that his two guests were well looked after by pleasuring them both during the night. Mike and Steven also saw to it that they once again satisfied each other by jerking each other off during the night.

When Mike and Steven awoke in the morning, Tom was not in the bed, and then Mike remembered that Tom had to be at the studio early that morning. He stretched out an arm and ran it over Steven's chest.

"Hi, my buddy."

Steven leaned across and kissed Mike. "Thanks for last night, it was really great."

"No I should thank you," said Mike. "That was one of the best fucks I've ever had," he said, letting his hand drop to Steven's limp dick and giving it a squeeze. Mike moved in the bed and gave a groan. "Oh, my back aches," he said.

"What's the matter?" asked Steven. "Is it too much sex?" he asked with a grin.

"I don't think it's enough," joked Mike. "No, I think it was from picking up those weights."

Steven got out of the bed, pulled the sheets down, admired Mike's body and said, "Right, up you get, I'm going to give you a massage. Come on, into the other room and onto that table."

Mike hauled himself from the bed and staggered through to the other room where Steven was waiting for him.

"Come on, up onto the bed you go. On your stomach," said Steven.

Mike climbed onto the bed and lay there waiting, his arms dangling over the sides of the bed. Steven had found some of Tom's aromatherapy oil and poured some onto Mike's back and legs. The scent from the oil wafted up their nostrils.

"Hmm, that smells great," said Mike, beginning to relax as Steven began to rub up the length of Mike's legs.

Steven worked on each leg taking his strokes right the way up to Mike's butt, then he moved to the side of the table and rubbed just near the entry to Mike's butt and over it.

Mike groaned in pleasure. "Ooh, that feels good," he said.

Steven continued his upward movement, now going to work on Mike's back and shoulders.

"Yes," said Steven, "I can feel the tenseness in your muscles here, you need to relax, but we'll sort it out."

Steven continued quietly massaging Mike's body and then he asked, "Are you in a relationship at all?"

Mike laughed, "No, but I would like to have one. Are you?"

"No," came the reply.

"Have you thought of going into a relationship with anyone, Steven?"

"Oh yes, I would love to, but somehow I haven't met the right person."

"I think you'd make someone very happy because you're such a caring person and that's the sort of person I'd like to be with," continued Mike, gently grunting as Steven exerted pressure on Mike's back.

Steven continued to rub Mike's back for some time, and then he moved back down to Mike's butt and ran his oily hands over it. As he did this, his hands slid into the crack of Mike's butt, opening his ass cheeks. He applied a little more pressure in this area and soon as his hands moved, so a thumb gently entered in Mike's asshole and then retreated. Steven repeated this a number of times, inserting first one thumb and then the other. Each time he did it, Mike raised his ass off the table to meet the pressure of his thumbs, and Steven's cock raised into the air a little higher. Just as Mike was beginning to enjoy this, Steven said, "Right, turn over."

Mike rolled over onto his back and had a stiff hard-on. Steven went to the foot of the bed and began to rub the front of Mike's legs. Again he worked the full length of them, right up to Mike's balls.

Steven looked into Mike's face and they smiled at each other.

"What are you thinking?" asked Steven.

"I was thinking about you," replied Mike. "I think you would make me happy."

Steven laughed.

"What do you mean by that?"

"I just think that there's a bond between us. I can't actually explain it but I find a very strong attraction to you. You are the type of person that I think I could get used to having around."

"Thanks, Mike, but could you see yourself in a relationship with a guy who works as a stripper in a club?"

"Steven, in my mind, a job is a job. I don't judge people by the work they do; I judge the person for who he is and I find you attractive, a pleasure to have around and I'm sure that I'd be very happy to live with you, that is, if you'd want to live with me."

Steven smiled back at Mike and continued with his massaging, without commenting on Mike's revelation.

When he had done both legs, again he moved to the side of the table. He poured some oil onto Mike's stomach and began to rub it in. He rubbed in Mike's pelvic area and in his groin, gently rubbing his balls as well. His hands lightly touched Mike's swollen dick and it reacted, but Steven didn't go further with it, instead he rubbed over Mike's belly and began to move up his chest. He massaged his shoulders and arms. As he lifted Mike's arms to massage them, Mike's hands brushed against Steven's hard cock, and each time Mike smiled.

"What are you smiling about?" asked Steven.

"Oh, nothing in particular, it's just that this feels good."

"The massage?"

"Yes, and this," said Mike dropping his hand to grab Steven's erection.

Steven began to move back down Mike's chest and headed towards his stomach again. This time when he neared Mike's hard-on, Steven ran his oily hands over its length. Mike groaned with pleasure as he did this. Steven then left that area and went to the bottom of the table where Mike's feet were. He held both Mike's feet and pulled Mike's legs open so that they were dangling over the sides of the narrow table. Mike tried to raise his head to see what was happening.

"Relax," said Steven.

He climbed onto the table between Mike's legs where they had been lying and stretched his muscular body down over the top of Mike's. Very slowly he began to massage Mike's body with his own, the oil rubbing onto his own chest, stomach, cock and legs. He pulled himself up to Mike's face and whispered when he got there, "I want you to slide that big oily dick of yours right up into my ass and I want you to fuck me as if this was the last day of your life."

Mike just grinned.

"I think I could get to like that," he said, holding onto Steven's firm ass.

Their cocks were sliding up and down each other as Steven worked his way over Mike's torso.

Steven pulled himself up Mike's body until he could feel Mike's cock touch the crack in his ass, then he slid back, causing Mike's huge cock to get pushed downward. He continued this for some while, getting Mike excited. Eventually, he repeated the movement, but instead, this time he held Mike's cock and slowly sank his ass onto it. He kept pushing until it was completely hidden in his ass. He held his position for a moment, just to get used to Mike's length and thickness, and then be slid up Mike's chest again sliding up his dick until just the cockhead stayed hidden. Just as Mike thought that Steven was going to let it slip out, Steven rammed his ass forcefully down onto Mike's dick causing Mike to gasp.

"Oh yes!" exclaimed Mike with pleasure. "Fuck my cock," he growled and Steven started a frantic riding and rocking motion.

Because of all the oil on their bodies, their movements were speedy and hard. Steven pounded at Mike's cock and Mike rose to every thrust that Steven gave- he was fucking him as though it was the end of the world. Here was this hunk of a man who had given him great pleasure the night before taking his ten inches and with no complaints. The sweat poured off their bodies and at times they nearly fell off the table, but Mike was determined to please Steven.

It felt like hours that they had been at it when Steven yelled, "I'm coming!"

"So am I," breathed Mike heavily, and both their actions speeded up more.

Their cocks exploded together, Mike filling Steven's bubble butt with his warm cum while Steven's cock erupted over Mike's chest. Steven was lying across Mike's chest as he began to shoot, causing his cum to be spread over both their bodies.

When they were emptied, Steven just lay in Mike's arms while they kissed each other, passionately. They looked into each other's eyes and smiled. After a little while, Steven sat up, still with Mike's cock in him and began to slide up and down its length again.

"You stay hard for a long time, Mike."

"I know. My friends always say it's because I'm so horny."

"You're also a bloody good fuck," said Steven.

"Thanks, so are you. In fact, you wouldn't like to come home with me when my holiday's over and live with me would you?"

Steven laughed. "Are you joking, or are you serious about the things you said?"

"Actually, I meant every word I said," replied Mike. "I think I'm falling for you in a big way and it's not just the brilliant sex."

Steven looked at Mike, deeply into his eyes. "You do really mean it, don't you?"

"Yes I do. I know we haven't got to know each other properly yet, and there's a mighty lot I still need to know about you, but I really find you very attractive and think that you've got a great personality, not to mention a great body."

"You want me to give everything up here?"

"What have you got to lose, Steven? You could easily get a job back home with your body and good looks and we could be together. Think about it. I could possibly help you get started in something."

Steven began to rock gently on Mike's still hard dick, which had not yet slipped from Steven's ass. He worked on it, riding up and down and covered Mike's body with kisses as he did so. Mike lay there luxuriating in the pleasure he was experiencing.

"Just lie still," said Steven, "I want you to enjoy this."

Steven worked on Mike's dick until he felt it swell again and Mike felt his balls lift up towards the base of his cock.

Mike smiled and then moaned, "Steve, I'm coming!"

"Come, my baby. Fill me with your love juice. Fuck this ass!" Steven's speed increased and Mike shot into his warm, comforting ass.

Mike took hold of Steven's cock and started jerking him off. Steven threw his head back and shouted as he reached his climax and let fly a thick wad of cum onto Mike's stomach. They lay together, exhausted. Once they had got their energy back, they went through to the bathroom and showered together, each washing the other's tired body. They then went through to the lounge and sat talking.

"Mike, would you really want me to go with you?"

"Yes, Steve, I meant it. I think in the short time that I've go to know you, I think that we have a lot in common."

"You mean sex!"

"That included," said Mike, "But I want you to know that I'm serious about this."

"Let me think about it and I'll get back to you," said Steven.

"Well I'll be here in Berlin for some time."

"Then where are you going?" asked Steven.

"I was hoping to go to Rome for a few days and then I'm off back to Amsterdam to catch my flight home," said Mike, "But it all depends on my nephew."

"You have a nephew here?"

Mike wasn't sure how to tell Steven about the whole episode with Barry, but then decided that if he mentioned something to Steven, he might also be able to help find Barry. Mike then proceeded to tell the whole story to Steven, who sat dumbstruck by what Mike had told him.

"And you never said anything to me before? We have to find him, then," said Steven, seeing Mike's anxiety about his nephew.

Mike was humbled by the enthusiasm and care for Barry that Steven was showing. This endeared the German man to him even more.

"I promised Tom that I would go to the studio today because I want to speak to one of the other actors there. I think he might know something of Barry's whereabouts."

"How long are you going to be in Rome and Amsterdam?" asked Steven.

"Two nights in Rome and then one night in Amsterdam."

"Well if I haven't given you an answer by the time you leave Rome, then I'm not coming," said Steven, "but I promise that I'll think long and hard about the offer you've made me."

"Fair enough, smiled Mike, "but I hope that the answer will be yes.

They dressed and headed back to Mike's hotel, where he changed into clean clothes and also gave Steven a clean change of clothes; then they went their different ways, Mike heading to the Galaxy studios.

When Mike arrived at the Studios, he slipped quietly into the building, knowing that they would be filming and he didn't want to upset the director again. He crept into the area where the sets were and saw Tom and the rest of the crew busy with a shot, so he waited out of sight of them until they had finished shooting their sequence. While Mike was watching what was going on, he overheard one of the sound technicians say something about 'the guy in the dungeon.' His mind flashed to Barry and wondered if they were talking about his young nephew.

"Cut!" reverberated around the room, as the director's voice boomed, and everyone took a breather.

"Tom!" whispered Mike, when Tom came near to where he was half hidden. "Over here!"

Tom moved to where he had heard Mike's voice coming from and found him hidden behind a rack of costumes.

"What are you doing here behind the costume rail?"

"I didn't want the director to see me, but while I was hiding here, I overheard the sound guy say something about, and I quote, 'the guy in the dungeon'. What dungeon or where is this dungeon?" asked Mike.

"Well I know there's a dungeon below this building where they used to keep old bits of scenery, but I don't think anyone goes down there."

"Do you think we can get down there without these guys knowing?"

"We can try, but I don't know when they're going to have a break, and even then, we'll have to be careful. Do you still want to speak to Kurt?" asked Tom.

"Yes, is that going to be possible?"

"It won't be a problem, but I'm worried that if he's connected to your nephew's abduction in some way, he might tell the others that we're onto them and then they'll either do something to your nephew or move him."

"So what do you suggest we do?" asked Mike.

Tom thought for a while and then came up with a possible solution to get Kurt on his own.

"Why don't we tell him that you want to have a private session with him and we take him down to the dungeon so you can plow that big cock of yours into his tight little ass," suggested Tom.

Mike laughed softly when he heard the suggestion, but as he nothing else to offer, he agreed with Tom's plan.

"And then, when I get him into the dungeon, what do we do?" asked Mike.

"Well, we can see if your nephew is in fact in the dungeon and if he is, then we get him out."

"And if he's not there?"

"Well, then you get Kurt's ass, but at the same time we might be able to get some information out of him."

Again, Mike gave a little chuckle, but agreed to Tom's suggestion.

"Leave it to me," said Tom, returning to the film set.

Mike watched as Tom made his way over to Kurt and whispered something to him. Mike could see the expression on Kurt's face; it was one of disbelief. He saw Tom point in Mike's direction and Kurt turned to look, but didn't see Mike, so he shook his head as though he didn't believe Tom's story. Mike could see this wasn't working, so he slipped out of his hiding place just long enough for Kurt to spot him. Kurt's face lit up when he saw Mike, because he knew now that Tom wasn't lying to him. Mike could see Kurt excitedly shaking his head and smiling broadly in anticipation of what was to happen. Just then the director called the actors back into their places. Kurt and Tom repositioned themselves with the others in their scene and the director shouted "Action!"

Mike watched from his secret hiding place and found himself becoming aroused by what he was seeing. Both Tom and Kurt were enjoying their performances and the former gave the young guy on the set, who Mike had not seen before, a blow job while Kurt slid his cock in and out of the young guy's ass. This went on for some time and then Mike heard, "Cut! Have a lunch break. Be back in an hour's time!"

Tom and Kurt left the set on which they were acting and pulled on some clothes. People who made up the crew started switching off lights and putting cameras in safe places and getting ready to have their break. The director was in deep conversation with his sound engineer and Tom and Kurt slid quietly and quickly from the studio, with Mike in hot pursuit. They scuttled down the stairway as quickly as they could, no one speaking. They reached the basement area and Kurt led Tom and Mike to a closed door. He pulled from his pocket a key and inserted it in the lock.

"Is it going to be safe here?" asked Mike, before they unlocked the door.

"Oh yes," replied Kurt. "Nobody ever comes down here except the director, and I don't think he's likely to make an appearance."

Mike looked at Tom who shrugged his shoulders as if to say he wasn't sure whether what Kurt had said, implicated him in the abduction or that Barry would be in the basement.

The key turned and Kurt opened the door. It was dark inside and they couldn't see anything, other than the light that was where they were standing. Kurt found the light switch and put on the light. Mike looked around him and saw that the basement was large and obviously covered a substantial area. There were old bits of scenery scattered all over the place. There were pieces of furniture, some tatty old costumes, spider webs and a musty smell that permeated throughout the basement.

"Come this way," said Kurt, leading Tom and Mike, further into the basement. "There's a bed here that we can use."

"Have you been down here before?" asked Tom.

"No," replied Kurt, becoming excited at the prospect of Mike making love to him.

Once more Mike and Tom made eye contact. If he'd never been down in the basement before, how did he know there was a bed there?

They followed Kurt and eventually came to a double bed that had a mattress but no sheets or blankets on it.

"Here we are," said Kurt, pulling down the shorts that he'd worn and leaping onto the bed, naked.

Mike and Tom stared at the young man lying spread eagled on the bed, his cock already beginning to become engorged.

Slowly and seductively, Mike played along by removing his shirt and then slowly unzipping his jeans. He pulled open the fly to his jeans to reveal a white pair of Calvin Klein briefs which encased his massive cock. Kurt licked his lips when he saw the whiteness of Mike's briefs and the bulge within them. Tom stood and watched the two men, but out of the corner of his eye he tried to see if he could see any evidence of someone having been there in the basement.

"Bring that massive weapon to me," cooed Kurt, thrusting his hips skywards.

Mike slid his jeans to the ground, stepped out of them, and then slowly removed his briefs. Kurt lay on the bed, his eyes growing wider as each inch of Mike's massive, hard cock emerged. Mike moved up closer to the bed and gently lowered himself on top of Kurt so that their cocks rubbed together, but Mike took Kurt's hands and move them above his head as he lay on his back. Mike pinned Kurt's arms and hands to the bed, then leaned closer to Kurt's face as though to kiss him. Kurt closed his eyes as he awaited the full lips of Mike, but instead when Mike neared him, he said, "Where is the young boy you've got captive here?"

Kurt's eyes flew open and he looked puzzled at Mike.

"What do you mean?"

Again, Mike leaned closer.

"You heard me, where's the young boy being kept?"

Mike ground his hard cock into Kurt as he asked the question.

"I don't know what you're talking about," replied a panic-looking Kurt.

"Tom! Bring me some rope or something to tie Kurt up," commanded Mike.

Tom had already pre-empted Mike's request and was standing by with some rope and thick cord, which he began using to tie Kurt's wrists to the bed-head. Kurt suddenly realized that his hour of pleasure was not going to be exactly as he had hoped. Once both Kurt's arms and legs had been securely fastened to the bed, Mike climbed off his prone body and stood at the side of the bed.

"Do you want to tell us about the young boy who's been taken prisoner? We think he's here, so you'd better start speaking."

"Help!" shouted Kurt, writhing on the bed and trying to break free.

Immediately Tom found a dirty piece of cloth which he stuffed into Kurt's mouth to gag him and prevent him from attracting attention. Mike slapped Kurt across the face and as he did so, he noticed how Kurt's cock throbbed and some pre-cum oozed from its tip.

"If you stop shouting, I'll remove the gag," shouted Mike, as he struck Kurt a second time.

Kurt's eyes showed fear in them, but Mike knew that somehow his young captive was enjoying the beating.

"Did you have something to do with the kidnapping?" sneered Mike, as he struck Kurt once more across the face.

Tears welled up in Kurt's eyes, then he nodded his head. Immediately Mike removed the gag.

"Now don't scream otherwise I'll really deal with you. Where's Barry?"

"Who?" sobbed Kurt.

"The young boy you took prisoner. Where is he?"

"Here," he sobbed.

"Here in the basement?" asked Mike. "Where?"

Kurt tried to point in the direction by using his head.

"Tom, you stay with this lout while I go and look for Barry."

Mike headed off in the direction that Kurt had indicated, moving scenery out of the way and climbing over rotting pieces of timber and cloth.

The basement covered a vast area, so Mike resorted to calling out Barry's name. As he continued moving further away from where he'd left Tom and Kurt, he heard what sounded like a groan. He stopped and listened again. Nothing was heard, so he called Barry's name again. Suddenly he heard the groan again and headed in its direction. He came across and pile of rubble and began removing it. Under the rubble, in what appeared to be a small opening, he found the bound and gagged form of Barry.

"Barry, are you OK?" asked Mike as he hurriedly ripped off the tape gagging Barry's mouth.

On seeing his uncle, Barry burst into tears and the two men hugged each other. Mike's still naked body warmed Barry and strangely, Mike felt himself becoming aroused as he held his young nephew close to him. Barry didn't appear to have any injuries on him, except for being tired looking and somewhat dehydrated. Mike untied his nephew and got him to his feet.

"How did you find me, Uncle Mike?"

"It's a long story my boy, but I'll tell you when we've got you out of here."

"You're naked!" exclaimed Barry, seeing Mike's aroused cock and realizing that Mike was indeed naked.

"That's another long story, and that I won't tell you."

Mike helped Barry back to where Tom was, pulled on his clothes again, but when Barry saw Kurt tied to the bed, his face became puzzled.

"I've seen you somewhere haven't I?"

Kurt didn't respond but lay quivering on the bed.

"Tom we need to get the police here immediately. Can I ask you to organize that for me while I keep and eye on Kurt? And get them to arrest the director, because I think he's involved in this."

Tom hurried out of the basement and headed for the foyer to phone the police while Mike and Barry remained with Kurt.

"I'd like to do to you what you did to my nephew, you scumbag, but I'm not going to give you the pleasure," said Mike, spitting venom from his mouth and striking Kurt as hard as he could across the face.

Barry merely stood and watched, not fully understanding why his uncle had behaved in this way.

"I don't understand," whimpered Kurt.

"Oh yes you do, so keep your lies to yourself."

It didn't take long for the police to arrive and together with Tom. They came into the basement to find Kurt still tied to the bed, naked. Once they had untied Kurt, Mike told them that they'd find the other accomplice upstairs in the studio and together with the police, Barry, Mike and Tom, went back up to the studio where they had great pleasure in seeing the film director arrested and taken away.

As they stood in the studio, Barry said, "I've been here, I remember this place, but there are some things that I can't remember. What happened here?"

Mike took Barry to one side, put his arm around the young boy's shoulder and then explained what had happened.

"You were obviously drugged, Barry and that's why there are certain things that you can't remember, and the reason why you thought you recognized that young guy that was arrested was because they had tied you to that bed over there," he said, pointing to the bedroom scene, "and that's where he had sex with you."

Barry remained unmoved. There was neither shock, nor repulsion. He merely stared at the bed, as though his mind was trying to relive the event that had taken place, then he turned to Mike: "May we go Uncle Mike?"

"Of course, but I need to make two phone calls first."

Mike picked up the phone in the reception area and dialed.

"Hi Pierre, it's Mike. I just wanted to let you know that we've got Barry and he's safe, so no ransom money needs to be paid."

"What about his captors?" asked Pierre.

"They've been arrested and are in custody here in Berlin."

"And you? Are you OK?"

"I'm fine thanks, and thanks for all your support and all the effort that you and the French police put in, I really appreciate it."

"I hope we're going to see you again," said Pierre, hoping that Mike might go back to Paris again.

"I'm not promising anything, because I'd like to take Barry on to Rome, but if we can, I'll try to come through Paris on our way home."

After completing his conversation with Pierre, Mike phoned Barry's family back in the States to tell them that he was safe.

Tom accompanied Mike and Barry back to Mike's hotel and while Barry had a warm shower to clean himself, Tom and Mike sat chatting.

"What's going to happen about Steven?" asked Tom.

"I don't know. That's up to him what he wants to do."

"But will you tell Barry about Steven?"

"Sure, why not. I think he's man enough to deal with his horny uncle's romances."

"So are you going to the club tonight?"

"Let me see how Barry feels, but I can't leave him alone, so if I do go to the club, Barry's going to have to come with me."

"Well, I'll leave you two guys alone, but if you decide not to go tonight, please contact me."

"Thanks Tom for everything," said Mike, giving Tom a hearty hug and kissing him tenderly.

When Barry came out of the shower with a bath towel wrapped around him he was surprised to see Tom gone.

"Where's Tom?"

"He's gone so we could have some time together," replied Mike, lying on the bed.

Barry moved over to the bed and lay down next to Mike. He lay staring at his uncle, tears again welling up in his eyes.

"What's the matter Barry?"

"I'm just so thankful to you and so happy to be with you. I'm sorry if I've caused you heartache and worry; it'll never happen again."

"Listen, when you're ready, you can tell me exactly what happened that night, but not now."

The two lay on the bed, their arms around each other and dozed off to sleep.

When Mike awoke, he was still clutching Barry to him and found that he had a hard-on, but so did Barry. Mike looked at the sleeping youth, worrying that he'd got himself a hard-on because of Barry, but he had to admit that Barry was a beautiful young man with a fine body. Just then, Barry's eyes opened and he smiled at his uncle.

"Hi," he whispered and smiled. Then blushing, Barry added, "and I think I've got a problem."

Mike roared with laughter and replied, "So have I."

Both men looked at each other's crotch, saw their erections and burst out laughing. They hugged and laughed, happy to be in each other's company and happy to be back together.

"Now listen, Barry. I have to tell you something."

"You've met someone, haven't you?" replied the young man.

"How did you know?"

"Is it your friend, Tom?"

"No."

"Pierre, the Frenchman?"

"No, but I have met someone here in Berlin. I'm supposed to meet him tonight, but I don't want to leave you alone here at the hotel, so I'll give him a miss."

"No you won't. You'll meet him tonight and I'll come with you. Somebody has to keep an eye on you," answered Barry.

Mike was touched by his young nephews, concern for him.

"But we're meeting at a club where he works and I don't know whether you'd like to be in a club like that."

"Like what?"

"You like dragging things out of me don't you?"

Barry giggled.

"Of course I do."

"It's like a strip club," replied Mike.

"I've never been to a German strip club before so it might be a good idea."

"Barry, this is not the usual strip club like you think of, it's a gay one."

"So?"

"I don't really know if you should. You wouldn't be offended after your ordeal?"

"Listen Uncle Mike, I'm not a kid you know."

Mike smiled at his upstart young nephew.

"You're right. You're a man and therefore, I'm no longer Uncle Mike, it makes me feel old. Call me Mike, or whatever you like."

"OK tart!"

"Tart!" exclaimed Mike in horror. "I'm no tart."

"Well with all the guys that I know you've seen I was beginning to think that you might be a tart."

"You know, you're pretty cheeky for a young upstart. You call me Mike."

"Whatever you say…Mike. Oh, and by the way, what's this new man's name?"

"It's Steven."

"And what's he like?"

"If you're coming with me tonight, you'll see him."

That evening, Mike and Barry prepared to go to the club. Mike noticed how excitedly Barry was at the prospect of going to a gay strip club. They arrived at the club, bought a couple of beers and watched as Steven and the others performed on the bar counters.

"So when's he coming?" asked Barry, whose eyes were everywhere.

"He's here already," replied Mike, knowing that his nephew was unaware of Steven's presence.

"So where's he?"

"Up there on the counter; the handsome guy with the tight jeans."

Barry looked at the dancers and became perplexed.

"Which one? There're quite a few with tight jeans."

"I told you. The handsome one."

Barry surveyed the group of men dancing, one by one and then turned to Mike.

"Is that him there?" asked Barry, pointing in Steven's direction.

Mike beamed, nodded his head and winked at Steven who was busy gyrating his body for both Barry and Mike.

"He looks quite nice," continued Barry.

"Nice!" exploded Mike. "He's fucking awesome, kid!"

Barry laughed at his uncle's devotion to the man, but he understood Mike's feelings.

Later Tom appeared for one of his strip performances, and Barry found himself swept up in the enthusiasm of the audience and was soon whistling and cheering as Tom removed his clothes. Mike watched Barry's reactions and smiled to himself. He was happy to see his nephew smiling and laughing once more. Perhaps his ordeal hadn't imprinted on his young mind and that he was in fact adult enough to cope with what had happened to him. In fact, during the strip, Tom even ventured to Barry and teased him as he removed his shirt. Mike watched enthusiastically as Barry took the teasing in his stride and went so far as to run a hand across Tom's bare chest.

When Tom had finished his act, both he and Steven came to join Mike, who introduced Barry to Steven.

"Barry, this is the guy I spoke to you about. This is Steven. Steven, this is the other man in my life, Barry."

The two shook hands and greeted each other.

"And I'm the other man in Mike's life," interrupted Tom.

"Of course, we can't forget Tom," said Mike, giving him a hug.

"I wondered who this hunky young man next to Mike was, that's why I chose to come to you during my routine," said Tom, admiring Barry.

They ordered drinks and while they were standing together, listening to the music being played, Mike asked the question to which he needed to hear an answer.

"Have you made a decision?" Mike asked Steven.

Tom was grinning from ear to ear when Mike asked. "Yes he has," he said, excitedly.

Mike looked lovingly into Steven's blue eyes, waiting for an answer. "So what's it to be?"

Steven smiled back at Mike and held his hand. "I'm coming with you, if you really want me."

Mike put down his drink and flung his arms around Steven's neck and kissed him on the mouth, their tongues searching each other. When they parted, he said to Steven, "You won't be sorry. I'll look after you, I promise."

"But I can't pack up here just yet. I'll have to give notice and then I'll join you," said Steven.

Barry could see the happiness in Mike's face and he was happy for his uncle. Drinks were ordered to celebrate Barry's recovery and Mike's new romantic attachment. The music continued to play and the four friends danced well into the night – even Barry joined in and thoroughly enjoyed himself in his new gay environment.

Back at the hotel that night, Mike asked Barry what he thought of Steven.

"The little I had to do with him and say to him, he seems quite a catch, but I hope you're going to be happy. I just hope you're doing the right thing."

"Meaning what?"

"Well, are you going into this relationship just for sex, or are your feelings strong enough to support him?"

"My feelings come first," replied Mike, "but yes, I do find him incredibly sexy."

"I can understand," said Barry, grinning.

"And that is supposed to mean what?"

"You have to admit that you like guys who are well-hung, don't you? And he fits the bill."

Mike laughed heartily at his young nephew's observation.

"For someone so young, you're quite observant, aren't you? Were you watching his dancing or the size of his package? But you're right."

"But you're not so small," added Barry.

Mike laughed at his nephew's comment.

"I'll let you into a little secret; you're quite a big boy yourself and I know a couple of people who admire what you've been blessed with," retorted Mike.

Barry looked aghast.

"What do you mean?"

"Remember I told you that someone had enjoyed sex with you, but you were drugged at the time, so you may not have realized. Well when you were lying on the bed, stretched out, I saw how big you actually were, and I must say I was most impressed."

"But how would you have seen me if you were in Paris and I was in Berlin?"

"Those guys who kidnapped you actually threatened to kill you. They thought they had someone else, but they'd made a mistake because you resembled the person they were after. Anyhow, they made a video of you being screwed by someone and that's when I saw you naked."

Barry blushed profusely as Mike told him the story.

"Who else saw it?" Barry asked timidly.

Mike smiled broadly.

"Pierre, me and the French police."

"What!"

Mike chuckled and added, "But they were all impressed with you."

Barry continued to blush at the thought of total strangers seeing him naked. The two then settled down to go to sleep, but not before Mike warned his younger nephew not to let his hands wander during the night.

The following day both Mike and Barry booked out of their hotel in Berlin, met up with Tom and Steven and made their way to the railway station to await their train to Rome.

Mike was like an excited school boy to see Steven again, and Barry shared some of his excitement. They stood and chatted alongside of the train until it was time to board. Barry thanked Tom again for the help that he had given to Mike in rescuing him, then he hugged and kissed Steven goodbye.

Tom kissed them both and said, "Now no funny business in Rome, OK?"

"I promise I won't fuck anybody," said Mike to Steven, "and nobody will fuck me. This ass is yours now, Steven, but what happens if I get horny while I'm in Rome?"

"Then you jerk off," said Steven.

"By the way, when are you going to meet me?" asked Mike.

"I'm going to tell my boss today, sort my things out, pack and then I'll meet you in Amsterdam, if all goes well" said Steven.

"I can't wait," said Mike hugging Steven to him. "I'm so happy."

"So am I," said Steven.

When the train pulled out of the station, all four waved feverishly and blew kisses to each other until Mike and Barry couldn't see Tom and Steven any more. Mike sat down on the seat in his compartment with a satisfied and contented grin all over his face and a warm feeling in his body.

Most of the journey, Mike just slept and when he wasn't sleeping, his thoughts were on Steven. Barry, on the other hand, had become like his uncle, an excited school boy. He was happy to be back with Mike and he'd realized the joy and happiness that his uncle had gained from his experiences in Europe. He sat smiling at the sleeping Mike and knew that they were being drawn ever closer to each other. He moved over to the seat on which Mike was sleeping and held Mike's hand in his, kissed his forehead and fell asleep resting his head against Mike's.

A Boner Book

ROME

The train pulled into the busy central station of the Eternal City and Mike and Barry disembarked and made their way on foot to their nearby hotel in the Via Achille Grandi. The place was simply furnished, but clean. They booked in, unpacked their bags and set off to see the sights of this ancient city.

They headed, first, for the famous Colosseum where they spent some time admiring these old remains from an ancient world, wondering what it must have been like being a gladiator.

"Forget the gladiators," said Barry, "what about the poor ones that got fed to the lions?"

"Would you fancy yourself as a Gladiator/" asked Mike.

"I don't know. It must have been a hard life to lead," replied Barry. "What about you?"

"I wouldn't mind a gladiator," said Mike, with a broad grin on his face.

"Trust you to misinterpret the question."

They wandered around the stone remains, trying to place themselves in the era in which the building was erected, and then headed towards the Vatican and a visit to the famous Sistine Chapel. Both Mike and Barry were awe inspired at what they saw, the beauty of the artwork and the buildings. Again, being in the building construction business, Mike appreciated the work that he saw.

"It's a pity we won't be able to get to Florence to see some of Michelangelo's other work," said Barry, looking up and admiring the ceiling in the Sistine Chapel.

"You just want to see the naked statue of David, don't you?"

"You're such a Philistine," chirped Barry. "Don't you appreciate good art?"

"Of course I do. It's just that I like teasing you."

They spent the whole day visiting the various tourist spots and being together, and then finally staggered back to his hotel, exhausted. They went up to their room, fell onto the bed and Mike immediately put through a telephone call to Steven.

"Hi, Steve, it's Mike. How are you?"

"I'm missing you already and you've only been gone a short time," said Steven.

"Don't worry," replied Mike, "it won't be long and we'll be together again."

"How's Barry doing?" enquired Steven.

"He seems to be fine," said Mike, turning to see his nephew. "We've spent the day together seeing most of the touristy places like the Colosseum and the Vatican, but we never saw the Pope, and now we've collapsed in the hotel room from exhaustion."

"I hope it wasn't exhaustion from anything you shouldn't have been doing?" questioned Steven.

Mike laughed. "Nothing like that. We've walked our feet off. We're going to have a little rest and then we'll go out and have something to eat. "

"I'm so looking forward to seeing you again."

"Me too, Steve, and what's more, I can't wait to get you home and proudly show you off to my family. In any case, they joked that I would bring back an Italian or a Frenchman; but they never banked on a sexy German."

"I hope they like me."

"Hey! What they choose to think is of no concern to me; it's more important that I like you."

"Like! Is that all?"

"Don't get cheeky with me," replied Mike, "Love, is more like it."

"That's better, because I feel the same way about you."

"Steve, I want you to know how much it means to me to have you in my life and for you giving up so much to be with me. I really do appreciate it and I love you for it."

"Mike, I wouldn't give up everything if I didn't feel the same about you and I'm actually looking forward to living in the US of A."

They spoke for about half an hour together, and then hung up.

Mike and Barry lay on the double bed that they had in their room, Mike now extremely content after his call to Steven, and soon fell fast asleep. At about seven that evening, they both woke up. Barry went to have a shower and then Mike followed. They both dressed and headed out for an evening meal and maybe a drink. They wandered down some of the small side streets passing a variety of bars and restaurants until they saw a pleasant looking restaurant. The two of them went in and ordered a meal and a glass of wine each with it. The young waiter who was serving them was very obliging and polite. He brought the wine, followed soon by Mike's plate of pasta and Barry's pizza. Mike sat eating his dinner and thinking of Steven and wishing that he were with him, although he was very happy to have Barry alongside of him. However, Mike seemed to go into deep thought because the young waiter came up to him and asked, "Are you OK, sir?"

This brought Mike back to reality.

"Oh, yes, I'm sorry. I was just thinking of somebody," said Mike.

"But you have somebody," replied the waiter, pointing to Barry.

Mike smiled at the young waiter and shook his head.

"No this is my nephew. I was thinking of someone else."

"He must be very lucky," smiled the young man.

Mike looked startled at the reference to 'he'; then he smiled at the young man. "No, I'm the one who's very lucky," said Mike.

"Were you thinking of Steven?" asked Barry.

Mike smiled and nodded.

"You really do like him, don't you?"

"I think this is the right person for me, Barry. I know that our meeting was in unusual circumstances, but somehow there's a bond between us. I can't exactly explain what I mean, but I know we have a connection."

They finished their meal and wine, paid the bill and left the restaurant. They continued to wander among the illuminated streets, looking at the people who passed by. Everyone seemed to be carefree and happy. Mike thought again of Steven and this made him happy. They went down the Via Merulana and turned into a side street. Mike saw a sign, which gave the name of a sauna. He stopped outside and thought of going in, but then he thought of Barry. Although he thought a relaxing sauna would do him good, he wasn't sure what to do about Barry.

Barry saw Mike looking at the sign and asked, "Do you want to go in, Mike?"

Mike turned to Barry, unsure whether to tell the truth or not, but before he could say anything, Barry spoke.

"Let's go in."

"You want to go for a sauna?"

"Why not? If I'm going to spend time with you, I might as well enjoy some of the things you enjoy."

"Do you know what can happen in places like this?" asked Mike.

"Tell me," replied Barry, acting almost coy.

"There are men there who might want to make a pass at you."

"I'd be very upset if they didn't," replied Barry.

Mike laughed at his nephew's audacity. Barry was very good looking and had a beautiful body, so yes, why wouldn't a man make a pass at him, but Mike was worried that it might affect Barry, especially after his abduction and rape.

"Are you sure?" asked Mike.

"Absolutely, and if I don't like a guy who's coming onto me, I'll just beat him up."

"Barry you can't just go around beating guys up because they look at you."

"I'm only joking, but remember what you promised Steven before we left Berlin."

"Don't worry, I haven't forgotten, but you know, you're beginning to sound like an old man keeping an eye on his son."

So it was agreed and they entered and paid.

The complex covered an area of three floors and was made up of a sauna, steam room, a Jacuzzi, relaxation areas, dark rooms and a labyrinth. Mike and Barry found their lockers, undressed and locked their clothes away. Both wrapped a towel around their waist and went to find the steam room. They walked together past a number of young men, all very Italian looking with olive skin, dark hair and equally dark mysterious looks.

Eventually they found and entered the steam room. They both found some space and sat down on the tiled step, stretched back and Mike closed his eyes. The warmth of the steam gave him a good feeling. He began to relax. There were about five people already in the steam room when they had entered, but Mike didn't really take much notice of them. He sat there, wiping the sweat and water off his body, with his mind back in Berlin.

It was the sound of heavy breathing that brought Mike back to the present. He opened his eyes and looked through the steam to where the sound was coming from. In a corner of the room he could see a group of men who were busy working on each other. He glanced in Barry's direction and saw that Barry was also watching the men. Mike watched them and began to feel the start of an erection as he visualized himself being part of their group activity. He promised Steven he wouldn't do anything untoward, he thought to himself.

The sounds from the men were becoming more intense and Mike knew that at least some of them were getting close to coming. He began to stroke the length of his big cock and felt its wetness from the steam, which made his hand movement slicker. Barry glanced down at what Mike was doing and saw the huge erection. Slowly Barry began to get a hard-on from watching both Mike and the men in the corner. Mike heard two of the men cry out and once they had shot their load, they left the sauna, leaving the other three. They continued to jerk each other off and Mike continued his slick hand movement on his own dick. One of the men saw what Mike was doing and gestured to him suggesting Mike join them. Mike thought about it and remained sitting. The same man looked at Mike again, but this time he saw the size of Mike's cock and immediately moved away from the other two towards Mike. He sat down next to Mike and took hold of Mike's cock. Mike wasn't sure whether to push the man's hand away, as he knew that Barry was watching, but wasn't part of the action. The man licked his lips and prepared to go down on Mike's cock with his mouth, but Mike stopped him. The man accepted that Mike didn't want to be sucked off, but he wasn't letting go. He wrapped both of his hands around the length of Mike's shaft, and slid both hands up its full length and then down again. Mike and Barry watched his actions and both were enjoying it; so Mike rested his back against the step behind him and let the man do the work. He worked on Mike's dick for quite some time until he could tell from Mike's breathing that he was about to shoot his load. Mike grunted and the first wad of cum shot up onto Mike's chest. The man increased the speed of his movement when he saw this, and Mike's cum flew over both of them. When Mike had finished, he wiped his chest with a finger, but before he could flick his cum onto the floor, the man took Mike's finger and put it into his mouth. The man sucked on Mike's finger, cleaning it of Mike's cum. He then rubbed his hand over the cum on Mike's stomach and his own, and licked it off his hand. Mike stood up, his cock waving in the air, wrapped his towel around his waist, which didn't hide his mighty hard-on, and left the steam room. Barry remained in the steam, horny as hell from watching the action performed on Mike. The same man who had pleased Mike, then turned to Barry, smiled at him through the steamy haze and lowered his head. Barry gasped as the warm mouth encompassed his young, hard, thick cock. He too lay back to enjoy the pleasure on offer much in the same way that Mike had done. It didn't take Barry long to get the pleasure that he had so desired. The man swallowed every last drop that Barry had to offer, wiped his mouth, thanked Barry in Italian and left the steam room. Barry went off to the showers and washed himself, then went to find a vacant rest cubicle. He found one, went in and lay down on the bed.

Mike had also gone in search of a quiet room in which to rest, found one and dozed off to sleep, thinking of Steven. He didn't know for how long he had slept, but woke to feel someone's mouth over his no longer flaccid cock. He turned to see who it might be and saw a dark-haired, dark-eyed young Italian boy of no more than about Barry's age. Mike looked at the young boy and thought of Tom back in Berlin.

Although the boy was young, Mike could tell that he was experienced in the use of his mouth and tongue. He exerted just the right amount of pressure on Mike's cock to give Mike an incredibly warm, lusty feeling. The boy held Mike's balls in his hand while his mouth worked up and down the length of Mike's cock. Every now and then, the boy gently squeezed Mike's balls and pulled them down between Mike's legs. The boy then climbed onto the bed and positioned himself between Mike's legs, burying his head over Mike's cock. The boy was trying hard to take the whole length of Mike's cock down his throat, but needed to relax his throat a little more to enable it to slide down his throat.

He kept up his action until he eventually relaxed his throat sufficiently to take Mike's full length. As he did so, Mike gasped in ecstasy and the boy's eyes went wide in anticipation. He held his position, savouring the taste of Mike's big cock, deep down his throat.

Although Mike had just recently emptied a load, the action from the young boy was bringing him closer to shooting another load. Once the boy had managed to take Mike's full length, he let go of Mike's balls and started to jerk himself off as he sucked Mike. The boy was getting closer because his breathing was loud and frantic, and his mouth was now working at double the speed it had been. Mike emitted a guttural grunt and fired into the young mouth that encased his cock. The boy swallowed and jerked at the same time. His mouth filled with Mike's hot cum and he groaned, "Hmmmmm!" He swallowed, but as he did, another load shot from Mike. The boy's own cum had shot onto Mike's legs and the bed. Mike kept shooting and thinking of Steven as he fired load after load down the throat of the young Italian. Eventually he stopped shooting and the young boy kept up his movement, draining every last drop from Mike. He raised his head from Mike's cock, wrapped a hand around the base of Mike's shaft and moved his hand up its length, squeezing it as he did. The last drops of Mike's cum oozed from the slit in the tip of his cock and the boy's tongue came out and licked it off. The boy kissed Mike's cock one last time, said "grazzi," and left the rest cubicle. Mike lay there for a moment and then dozed off to sleep again. He awoke with someone calling him.

"Sir, we are closing. It is time for you to go."

Mike wiped his eyes, rose, and went in search of Barry, whom he found lying in a cubicle not far from where he had been, then they had a quick shower, dressed and together they made their way through the streets of Rome back to their hotel.

Back at the hotel, Barry and Mike lay naked on the bed next to each other, both staring up at the ceiling and neither saying anything. Eventually, Mike spoke first.

"What are you thinking of Barry?"

For a moment, Barry remained silent.

"I was just thinking of everything. You know, the kidnap, you finding me and tonight."

"What about tonight?" queried Mike, looking at Barry in wonder.

Barry turned towards Mike.

"Tonight was fun. I had a great time. Thanks Mike."

"Why thank me, I did nothing, except go for a sauna."

"But I enjoyed it."

Then Mike smiled more to himself.

"Did you score there?" asked Mike.

Barry blushed.

"You know the guy who jerked you off, well he took me after you left."

"And?"

"And what?"

"Well did you do anything?"

"He did."

"Well, what did he do and did you enjoy it?" asked Mike.

Again Barry blushed.

"Of course; he gave me a blow job, but don't tell Mum when we get home."

Mike sniggered and said, "Of course I wouldn't. If I did, she'd never allow us to see each other in case I corrupted you."

"I was corrupted years ago at high school."

"You were? By whom?"

"One of the football team players; in the locker room."

This made Mike almost howl with delight at this revelation.

"Does she know?"

"Of course not. I couldn't even tell you."

"Thanks for the trust," said Mike in mock hurt.

"I didn't know if you'd tell Mum."

"Barry, I think you should know me by now. If you tell me something that's confidential, it remains a secret and I don't say a word to anyone, so whatever happens on this trip, other than your kidnapping, I won't tell a soul."

"Thanks, Mike," said Barry, leaning across the bed and giving Mike a kiss on the cheek.

The following day, Mike decided that he was not going to go out that night, but rather stay in at the hotel and watch TV, but during the day he decided he wanted to take a trip to Naples to visit the island of Capri and asked Barry if he wanted to join him, to which the young agreed.

They set off for Naples, taking their bathing costumes and towels with them, in the hopes of having a swim in the sea. When they arrived in Naples, they caught a hydrofoil to Capri and began a tour of the island. The beauty that confronted them was outstanding. The views were stunning and Mike wished that he had Steven with him to share the beauty.

Mike spotted an Italian man of about thirty with a small boat and persuaded him to take Mike and Barry to visit the Blue Grotto. The man agreed and they set off, the man rowing his boat slowly through the sea. Mike decided that he might as well try to get a tan while he was being rowed to the cave, so he took off his T-Shirt and shorts. Barry followed suit. They both stretched out in the rowing boat in their Speedo costumes and let the sun bake down on them. The Italian man looked at Mike and than at Barry and said something in Italian, which Mike didn't understand.

"I don't understand," said Mike in English.

The Italian repeated what he had said, but this time he pointed at Mike. Mike was still unable to understand, so he shrugged his shoulders and shook his head as if to say that he didn't understand. Mike asked Barry if he knew any Italian.

"Not a word, I'm afraid."

Eventually, the Italian, in desperation, once again pointed at Mike and in very broken English said, "Big!"

Mike looked down at his crotch, smiled at the man and nodded, "yes."

Barry giggled and the man looked at Barry's crotch. He smiled at Barry.

"Big too!"

The three continued their journey with no one speaking. After some time, they arrived at the beautiful Blue Grotto. Mike's breath was taken away when he saw its beauty and he wanted to swim in the grotto.

"Can we swim in here?" he asked the man.

The man didn't understand, so Mike mimed a swimming action and pointed to the clear water. This time the man understood, smiled and nodded. Mike dived overboard into the cool water and Barry soon followed. The man tried to keep the boat from floating away from the two men while they swam in the clear water. When they had both cooled down and were ready to get back in the boat, they swam over to it and the man put out a hand to help Mike and then Barry back in. Mike climbed in and sank onto the bench opposite the rower. Barry followed and resumed where he had been sitting in the boat.

"Thank you," said Mike.

The man smiled, pointed at Mike's dick again and said, "Still big!"

Mike looked down and saw that his wet Speedo costume clung to his skin and revealed the full length, the thickness of his shaft and the outline of its cut head.

The Italian grasped his crotch and said, "Small!"

Mike simply smiled back at the man and put his hand inside his Speedo to adjust the lie of his cock. The whole time, the man never took his eyes off Mike's cock, except occasionally to see if Barry's crotch was also still "big!". He placed the oars into the boat, stood up, causing the boat to rock and roll, unzipped his pants and pulled out his uncut cock. Mike didn't know where to look or what to do. Barry quietly giggled behind his hand. Both could see that the man was right – he didn't have a big dick, but he was frantically trying to get it bigger. He jerked himself, possibly hoping that Mike or Barry would assist him, but neither Mike nor Barry moved, nor did their cocks. By this time Barry was causing the little boat to rock and roll with his laughter, but Mike maintained a straight face, trying desperately not to laugh. After about two minutes of this, the man realized that neither Mike not Barry were going to co-operate so he put his small dick back into his pants, zipped up and started rowing the boat again, mumbling to himself in Italian as he did so. As they exited the cave into the sunlight, Mike once again stretched out his body to dry his Speedo and to tan, alongside of Barry.

When they arrived back at the harbour, Mike paid and thanked the man, who looked as though he was ready to burst into tears at what he had lost and what he had not been able to touch.

After spending a wonderfully relaxing day on Capri, they made their way back to Rome, arriving there in the early evening. Back in the hotel, Mike again put through a phone call to Steven.

"Hi, my baby! How's it?"

"Hi, Mike, how are things?"

"Barry and I have just come back from Capri, which was so beautiful, I just wanted you to be there, but instead we had a horny little Italian boatman who was after my cock."

Steven roared with laughter, loud enough for Barry to hear it over the phone. "Are you so desperate that you're going after little Italian boatmen now?"

"You don't have to worry, nothing happened. It's just that I had a swim and of course when I got out of the water my Speedo clung to my body and showed up my cock and he wanted a piece of it."

"I hope you didn't give him any of it," said Steven.

"Trust me he got nothing from either of us, except a half erection of his own, if you could call it that, trying to jerk off in the boat."

Steven once again roared with laughter. "You mean he was jerking off in the boat?"

"Yep," said Mike, also laughing. "But I must tell you that last night Barry and I went for a sauna to relax and we quite enjoyed it."

"Barry went!"

"Yes, and he thoroughly enjoyed himself."

"Is he ...?"

"Hm, I think maybe."

"And did you score there?" asked Steven.

"I promise, nobody got this ass, and my cock didn't get anybody else's ass. I jerked off once in the steam room and then when I was sleeping in a cubicle, a boy of about eighteen or nineteen came in and sucked me off and then left."

"I hope that was all," said Steven.

"You can ask Barry, if you don't believe me."

"Put him on the phone."

Mike handed the receiver to Barry.

"Steven wants to speak to you."

"Hi Steve, how are you?"

"I'm fine thanks Barry, but I hear you've been misbehaving."

"No, not really, just having some fun."

"And did you enjoy your fun?"

"Yep, it was good, and it's true what Mike says, he didn't allow anyone near his you know what."

"The word is ass, Barry. And remind Mike that if anyone gets into his ass or he gets into anyone else's, then I'm not coming to Amsterdam. Tell him that."

Barry laughed and repeated the message to Mike. Mike snatched the phone from Barry.

"You know I'd keep my promise to you, but talking of Amsterdam, we'll be getting there at about five in the afternoon," said Mike.

"OK," said Steven, "I'll meet you at the hotel you told me about, and then we can plan something to do. Now don't run up this phone account, you know how hotels over- charge on phone calls, so hang up."

"I like the idea of planning something to do," laughed Mike.

"Now hang up. You've only got one thing on your mind."

"Yes, and that's you. I'll see you in Amsterdam, babes," said Mike.

"Cheers my buddy. I can't wait to see you."

Mike put down the phone and lay on the bed thinking of Steven and rubbing his hand over his cock, while Barry watched, smiling to himself.

"You really are horny for him aren't you?"

"Does it show?" enquired Mike, still massaging his ever-growing erection.

Barry chose not to reply to that question, but as they lay on the bed watching TV, Mike slowly reduced his hand movement until he stopped massaging himself.

"That's better," commented Barry.

"I beg your pardon, what were you saying?"

"Your mind has been in your crotch since that phone call and you've only just got back to earth again."

The two laughed together

As they were leaving Rome the following day, they had decided to have an early night so that they would be fresh for when Mike met with Steven. As they lay on the bed watching a boring film on the TV Mike thought of going out for a while, but then he thought instead of having dinner in his room and just going to sleep.

"Do you feel like room service tonight, Barry?" asked Mike.

"I don't have a problem with that. Where's the menu?"

Mike grabbed the room service menu and between them they searched through it for something to eat. Once they had decided on what to eat, they called for room service.

Mike ordered their meal from the menu that was in the room and a beer each.

"While we wait, I'm going to have a shower then you can have one," said Mike, jumping off of the bed.

Mike went into the bathroom to have a shower, leaving Barry lying on the bed watching TV.

Mike peeled off his clothes and left them in a pile on the chair in the room. His muscular body moved silently across the carpeted bedroom floor, his heavy dick swaying from side to side while Barry watched him. He entered the bathroom and turned on the shower taps. He stood admiring his body in the bathroom mirror as he waited for the water to heat to the right temperature. Slowly the mirror began to mist up and he knew then that the water was the right temperature. He entered the shower and let the warm water run over his body. It hit his head and poured down over his face and chest, continuing over his stomach and down his legs, with some making a detour to run down the length of his cock. He leaned forward slightly allowing the water to run down his back and over his ass. He felt its warmth trickle between his ass cheeks and he leaned even further forward. As he felt the warm water running over his ass, he pulled his ass cheeks apart to allow the water to run over his asshole, which caused a warm feeling inside of him. He felt his cock begin to rise and swell. After some time, he turned to face the waterspout and allow the stream of water to fall onto his slowly rising cock. It seemed like a battle between his ever-increasing cock and the water stream, as his cock rose and the water tried to force it downwards.

After some time of luxuriating under the shower of water, Mike switched it off, stepped out of the shower and wrapped a towel around his waist. He made his way back into the room and told Barry he could go and shower, now that Mike was finished. Barry stripped off his clothes and made his way into the bathroom, closing the bathroom door behind him. Mike once again heard the water being switched on.

Just then Mike heard a knock on his bedroom door. He crossed the carpeted floor, leaving wet footprints as he went, and opened the bedroom door.

"Good evening, sir. You ordered room service!" said a rather surprised young man with black hair and piercing pale blue eyes. He stood staring at Mike's wet and half naked body, not quite knowing what to say or do next.

Mike watched his face. The man's eyes met Mike's, and then wandered over Mike's muscular chest and down to the towel around Mike's waist. When his eyes reached that section of the towel, which was bulging out from Mike's half erection, his eyes widened and his mouth fell open.

"I think you'd better come in," said Mike, " I don't think any body wants to see me half naked?"

The young man, who looked no older than his early twenties, pushed the dinner trolley into the bedroom, still finding it very difficult to remove his eyes from Mike's bulge. Of course, Mike realized this and found that his half erection was growing, the more the young man looked at it.

"Are you signing for this, or paying for it?" asked the young man.

"I'll sign for it," said Mike, crossing to the dressing table to pick up a pen in order to sign. The young man hustled behind him and as Mike turned, having picked up his pen, he bumped into the young man, who felt Mike's hard cock against his own. The two men stood staring at each other, Mike's hard cock up against the young man.

"I'm terribly sorry, sir," said the young man.

"Oh, that's quite alright," said Mike, "I don't think you did any damage, but perhaps we'd better take a look and check."

Mike released the towel from his waist, letting it fall to the ground and revealing his throbbing hard-on.

"Oh my God!" exclaimed the young man.

"Does it look damaged to you?" asked Mike.

"No, sir," stammered the young man, looking embarrassed.

"Maybe you'd better feel it and see that nothing's broken."

The young man tentatively stretched out a hand but as soon as it neared Mike's cock, he withheld touching it.

"I think that perhaps it's been damaged internally from where you bumped into me, and the only way it's going to be healed is if you kiss it better," said Mike smiling in a teasing manner and crossing over to the bed.

Mike sat himself on the edge of the bed, facing the young man, with his cock swaying erect in the air. The young man slid a hand down to his crotch and squeezed his own cock hidden within his black pants, as he smiled at Mike. He crossed the floor to where Mike was sitting.

"Is it sore, sir?" he asked.

"Very," replied Mike, screwing up his face in mock agony. "But I'm sure that you can make it better."

The young man gently ran his fingers through Mike's hair and down the back of his neck; then he sank to the floor on his knees. He looked up into

Mike's face and smiled. He looked down at the waiting 'patient' and opened his mouth. His lips met the tip of Mike's cock and he wrapped them around the top allowing his tongue to run over Mike's piss slit. He then began to kiss his way down the length of Mike's shaft. Mike lay back onto the bed, allowing the young man full access to his swollen dick and balls. The young man's tongue was experienced and worked on the 'healing processes of Mike's 'injury'. Throughout all this, the shower water continued to spatter onto Barry's body and the bathroom floor.

"Take all of it," sighed Mike.

The young man obliged, sending Mike's cock to the back of his throat and holding it there for a moment before rising up its length again. After a while, the young man moved onto Mike's balls and gently massaged them with his tongue and mouth. As he was doing this, he unbuttoned his shirt and pulled it off. Mike looked up from his position and saw a beautifully defined young body. He watched the actions of the young man, which resembled those of a professional, as he kept working on Mike's cock while he unbuttoned his pants and slid out of them, taking his briefs off at the same time.

He lathered Mike's cock with his mouth and tongue, making it wet and slippery. When the young man had made Mike's cock very slippery, he rose and for the first time, Mike was able to see the young man's long, slender, uncut cock. The young man moved closer to Mike and positioned himself over Mike's throbbing wet cock and slowly lowered himself towards the tip of Mike's cock. Mike watched with anticipated ecstasy for the young man to ride his rod, and suddenly remembered his promise to Steven that he wouldn't fuck anybody and nobody would fuck him. Was he to break that promise? Steven need never know, he thought. But what if Barry came out of the bathroom and saw the young man riding Mike's cock, what would he say to Steven then? That ass looks good to fuck, he thought. He felt the tip of his cock touch the entry passage of the young man. All he had to do was push up into the young man and he could be in heaven. He felt the young man's sphincter on his cock.

Mike suddenly pushed the young man's body up and away from his cock. "No," he said.

"But you want it," said the young man.

"Yes I do, but I can't," said Mike.

"Why not?"

"I promised my lover that I wouldn't fuck anybody other than him."

"But I damaged you and I must make it better," said the young man.

"Well, actually, it's not that badly damaged," said Mike.

"May I still kiss it better?" requested the young man.

"By all means," said Mike, with a tone of relief in his voice as he said it.

The young man's mouth went to work, frantically rising up and down Mike's shaft. As his mouth set to work, so his fingers, which he had wet, moved around Mike's puckered pink target. He slipped two fingers into Mike's asshole and twisted them around inside, causing Mike to sigh with pleasure and thrust his hips upwards. The young man began to enjoy this because the more that he moved his fingers around, the more Mike fucked his mouth. With his free hand, he grasped Mike's balls and squeezed them. He could feel them beginning to rise towards the base of Mike's cock, and Mike let out a growl of passion as he shot one load after another into the young man's mouth. The young man tried to swallow as fast as he could, but Mike had a heavy load and the young man couldn't contain it all. He kept moving up and down Mike's length but cum was now spilling from his mouth as he did so, running down Mike's cock. When Mike had finished shooting, the young man removed his mouth from Mike's cock and settled his tongue on Mike's balls and began to lick the cum from there.

Mike sat up and pulled the young man onto the bed next to him, flipped him onto his back and lowered his mouth onto the young man's dick. Mike nibbled at his foreskin, pulling it with his teeth and thrusting his tongue under its cover. The young man groaned as Mike did this to him. While Mike was sucking the young man, he was busy working on his own cock, getting it fully hard again. When he felt it was fully erect, he swiveled himself into a sixty-nine position above the young man and lowered his cock into the young man's waiting mouth. The water in the bathroom stopped flowing, but neither Mike nor the young realized this. Mike buried his head between the young man's legs and licked his balls and moved around to his asshole with his tongue. When he had wet it sufficiently, he gently inserted a couple of fingers to give the young man the same pleasure that he had received. As he did this, the young man bucked forcing his slim cock deep into Mike's throat. This turned Mike on and he thrust downwards into the young man's throat.

The handle to the bathroom turned and the door opened ever so gently. Barry peered out and saw Mike busy on the bed, so he gingerly closed the door but not completely. Barry was able to look through the tiniest of cracks and witness Mike at work.

Mike could feel himself getting closer again, but this time he didn't want the young man to suck him off, so he pulled out of the young man's mouth and positioned himself so that his cock was facing the tip of the young man's cock. Mike placed the cut head of his dick at the tip of the young man's, and, taking hold of the young man's foreskin, he pulled it so that it encompassed the head of his dick. With both their cock-heads docked and touching each other, and completely encased in the young man's foreskin, Mike took hold of both their cocks and started jerking them off. It wasn't long before they both reached their climax and began to shoot. Mike held onto their cocks tightly, not allowing any of the cum to shoot out, and watched as the hood of the young man's cock filled and swelled with their hot cum. When they had exhausted their supplies, Mike let go of the young man's cock. His foreskin rolled back forcing their combined cum to ooze from them onto their cocks. The young man rubbed their cum over his stomach and over Mike's. Mike collapsed onto the bed next to the young man and lay there panting.

"Now you'll have to have another shower," said the young man, "and your dinner is probably cold."

"That's OK," said Mike, "I think I've had enough to eat tonight," he said, giving the young man's hand a squeeze, "and I think you've made my cock better," he laughed.

The young man rose from the bed and began to dress, while Mike went to see if his dinner was possibly warm. When the young man was dressed, he crossed to Mike, gave him a kiss on both cheeks and said, "Your lover, he's a very lucky man to have someone like you."

"Thank you," said Mike. "Do you have a lover?"

"No," replied the young man, " I like to keep everybody happy."

"Well you do a very good job," said Mike.

At that, the young man beat a hasty retreat from the room. Once Barry had heard the bedroom door close, he emerged smiling from the bathroom. He smiled down at Mike who by now was exhausted and was sitting on the edge of the bed.

"I see dinner has arrived."

"Yes," replied Mike, looking flushed.

"But I think you've eaten, haven't you?" continued Barry, smiling even more broadly.

"You little shit!" roared Mike. "You were watching, weren't you?"

Barry laughed and sat down on the bed next to Mike.

"You're pretty good, you know."

"Thanks for the compliment, but you're still a little shit."

They ate together and then climbed into bed to continue watching the boring TV programs that were on offer. Eventually, they switched off the bedroom light and settled down to sleep. Mike lay on his back thinking of

Steven.

"What are you thinking of?" asked a voice in the dark.

"Need you ask?"

"And what would you tell Steven about the room service tonight?"

"We had room service, that's all."

Barry giggled.

"Is that what you call it?"

"Shut up and go to sleep!"

Barry snuggled up closer to Mike, put an arm around his waist and felt himself becoming hard.

"Are you getting a hard-on?" questioned Mike.

"Maybe," was the reply.

"Just remember, my ass is not available to you."

Mike lay there feeling Barry's cock growing harder and longer, until he stretched out a hand and felt it.

"Are you feeling horny?" Mike asked.

"Yep. It was from watching you, Mike."

Gently and seductively, Mike began to stroke Barry's long, thick cock. Barry clasped onto Mike and sought Mike's burgeoning cock. When he felt it growing, Barry reciprocated by stroking it gently as well. Both men sought the other's mouth and when they made contact, Barry's tongue forced its way into Mike's mouth and began to search its contents. Their lips stayed glued to each other as their bodies ground into each other. Their passion for each other was deep and the love they had for each other was even deeper. Their breathing increased and almost silently, they emptied their love on each other. When eventually their bodies began to settle back to rest, their lips still maintained contact until Barry broke free from Mike's arms and he smiled in the dark at his soul mate.

"Thanks Mike," whispered Barry, as he dozed off to sleep.

The following day, Mike and Barry caught their flight to Amsterdam, on the last leg of their eventful holiday. As they sat on the Boeing from Rome, Mike thought of his holiday and how things had happened that he had never planned to happen, but that's what makes a holiday such fun, he thought. First, he had met a beautiful person, in the form of Steven, who was now going to be part of his life, and second, there had been so many terrific people and places that he had come into contact with, that he was over the moon, and third, he had discovered a special bond between himself and Barry, which he treasured.

He lay back in his aircraft seat, closed his eyes and thought beautiful thoughts.

A Boner Book

THE LAST LEG

Their flight landed at Schiphol Airport and they made their way into the center of Amsterdam to the hotel near the Leidseplein that Mike had stayed at when he first landed there. When they arrived at the reception desk, he was virtually overwhelmed by Hans who was so glad to see him again.

"Hans, is there any chance of getting two rooms, please?"

"For you, dear Mike, we'll always find ... TWO!" said the startled Hans.

"Yes, my friend, two. One for me and one for my best friend here," he said, pointing to Barry. Hans was a little surprised to see Barry.

"Hans, let me introduce you to my favorite nephew, Barry. Barry, this is Hans. You need to watch out for him because Hans could lead you astray."

Hans and Barry shook hands and both laughed at Mike's snide comments.

"By the way, Hans, I'll be expecting a friend later in the day," said Mike, smiling from ear to ear.

"From the expression on your face, I would say that this must be some special friend, huh?"

"Very special," grinned Mike, " he's my new partner, hopefully for life."

"OK, so where did you find him and what's his name?"

"His name's Steven and I met him in Berlin."

"German!" exclaimed Hans. "I know all about them. I believe they make good lovers and have big dicks," he whispered as though Barry shouldn't hear.

"Is that all you think about?" asked Mike, "big dicks?"

"Well don't you?"

"Sometimes," said Mike.

"Well, does he have a big one?" asked Hans, with a cheeky smile.

"Yes, but I love him for who he is and not for his dick," replied Mike.

"Oh yes, I've heard all those clichés before, but seeing that it's coming from you, I'll believe you. So when do I get to meet him?"

"This evening, and I don't want any nonsense from you tonight."

"What nonsense would I give?" questioned Hans, looking hurt by Mike's comment.

"You know what I mean," replied Mike.

Hans turned to where the room keys were kept, picked up a key and dangled it seductively in front of Mike.

"Room 14, the honeymoon suite for you! You can go up to the room if you like, but I'll be up later with a surprise," said Hans, with great delight. "For you Barry, here's the key to room 16. It's on the same floor, just across the hallway, and if you want a surprise, I can come up to you as well."

"You see, I told you we had to watch him, Barry. Hans, I don't want you barging in when Steven and I are there, OK?"

"Would I barge?" came the reply. "Please, I have respect for you."

Mike simply shook his head and laughed. He picked up his luggage and went to find room 14 while Barry followed closely up the staircase to room 16.

When Mike entered the room, he found it simply, yet very tastefully furnished and in the center of the room was a double bed on which Mike collapsed. He lay there, staring up at the ceiling and then burst out laughing. As he laughed, he saw himself laughing back from the roof of the room, as the honeymoon suite had a mirror on the ceiling. This was quite kinky, he thought, being able to make love on the bed and watch yourself at the same time. He got up off the bed and looked around the room. On the wall adjacent to the bedroom door was a dressing table with a mirror attached to the wall, and next to that were two easy chairs covered in rich, red-coloured brocade, which matched the curtains. Also in the room were a TV set and a low coffee table on which were a number of gay magazines. Just then, there was a knock at the door and in came Hans.

When Mike saw him, he burst out laughing and said, "What is this room?"

"I told you, I was giving you the honeymoon suite!"

"But what's with the mirror on the ceiling?" asked Mike.

"It adds to the fun," replied Hans, with a twinkle in his eyes. "If you don't like it, I'll move you to another room."

Mike thought about the offer and said, "No thanks, I think we'll stay here."

"I thought you would," smiled Hans. "Now here's the surprise I promised you,"

and from behind his back he produced a bottle of champagne, which he handed to Mike. "For the newly weds!"

"Gee thanks, Hans, but you didn't have to, you know."

"I know, but I want you and Steven to have a memorable honeymoon," said Hans.

"Well, I don't want to waste any of your time, because I'm sure that you want to have some rest, after all, you won't get much tonight, so I'll leave you to your mirror and your bed and send your lover up to you when he arrives."

At that, Hans swept from the room, leaving Mike to wait for Steven, and made his way to Barry's room to see if he had settled in. Hans knocked on the door and Barry shouted "Come in!" Hans opened the door to find Barry busily unpacking his bags wearing only his white briefs.

"Ooh! I'm sorry," said Hans, in fake shock.

"Oh, hi. Come in Hans."

Barry turned to see Hans and Hans saw a magnificent sight in front of him.

"Hmm!" cooed Hans. "You are just like Mike."

"I don't understand," replied Barry.

"Big," was all Hans would say. "I just wanted to check that you had settled in OK."

"Yes, thanks Hans."

"Well, if Mike is too busy with his new lover tonight, then maybe I could show you around Amsterdam, if you'd like that."

"Thanks very much. That's very kind of you but let's see what they're going to do."

"I have a pretty shrewd idea what they're going to do," sighed Hans.

In the meantime, Mike had unpacked his luggage, taken off his clothes and then flung himself onto the bed and lay staring up at the mirror on the ceiling. He lay there admiring his body and running his hands over its contours, feeling his nipples and then letting his hands run down the length of his cock. His hands grasped around his balls and he squeezed them, then he thrust his hips up into the air. He found himself getting turned on by his own image in the mirror. He then rolled over onto his stomach and turned his head so that he could see his back view. He thrust his butt into the air and looked proudly at his firm, rounded buns. After a while, Mike simply lay on the bed on his stomach and dozed off to sleep.

Barry, in the meantime completed unpacking his bag and also lay down on his bed, but he had no mirror into which he could stare.

Later in the day, Steven arrived at the hotel dressed in tight leathers and a white T-shirt, and introduced himself to the person at reception, who happened to be Hans.

"Hi," said Steven, " I have a friend who was booking in here today and I was to meet him here."

"His name doesn't happen to be Mike?" asked Hans.

Steven looked surprised. "Yes, as a matter of fact it is."

"Then you must be Steven," said Hans. "We were expecting you. I hope that you had a pleasant journey?" asked Hans, sizing up the young German from top to toe.

"Yes, thanks very much, but who told you about me?"

"Oh, Mike has told me everything, and he's so looking forward to seeing you again. Come, let me take your luggage for you and I'll take you up to the room," said Hans picking up Steven's luggage.

They made their way up the steep stairs until they reached the door to the honeymoon suite. Hans didn't knock, but put the extra key in the door and opened it. The sight that greeted his eyes was very pleasing, not only to him, but also to Steven. Mike was lying fast asleep on his stomach on the bed, naked.

"I'll leave you here," whispered Hans, handing the spare key to Steven.

Steven quietly closed the door behind him and put down his luggage.

Hans, in the meantime, had rushed into the room next door to the honeymoon suite and stood in front of the 'window' in the room. This 'window' happened to be the reverse side of the mirror on the wall of the honeymoon suite. Unbeknown to Steven and Mike, they had a one-way mirror on the wall in their room. Hans watched as Steven quietly pulled off his T-shirt to reveal a well-toned, muscular body. Steven then ran his hands over his crotch in his leather pants. He then unbuttoned the top button and slowly slid the zip down. As he did so, Hans could see that Steven didn't have any briefs on underneath his leathers. Steven put a hand into his leathers, under where his balls were and Hans watched as Steven's hand unloaded a huge dick with heavy, bulging balls that fell and hung loosely when he released them. Hans immediately started playing with himself in his pants.

Steven wriggled his hips as he pushed his leathers down his legs onto the floor and stepped out of them. He stood at the base of the bed between Mike's open legs, pulling on his long cock, getting it harder. As he did this, so Hans had pulled out his dick, which was already hard, and he was pulling on it.

Once Steven's cock was fully erect, he gently lowered himself onto Mike's back so that his cock was able to rub in the crack between the cheeks of Mike's bubble-butt. When Mike felt this, he stirred, but didn't look around.

"Cut it out, this is only available for Steve and no-one else," said Mike, sleepily.

Steven carried on rubbing his thick dick up and down Mike's butt.

"I said, cut it out!" exclaimed Mike, turning to see who was busy on him.

When he saw it was Steven, he flipped Steven from his back, flipped himself over and lay there hugging and kissing Steven.

"Oh it's so good to see you again, Steve."

"It's great to see you, babes, and it's great to hear that you won't allow anyone else have access to this beautiful ass of yours."

Nobody said much after that because they were too busy making up for lost time. All the time, Hans stood in the room next door, watching the honeymoon couple make love, while he jerked himself off.

Steven slid his well-licked cock into Mike's waiting butt and began to pound into its depths. The bed bounced as Steven beat his meat into Mike's pink hole, pushing its full length down only to be met by Mike's upward thrust. Mike raised his ass into the air and Steven climbed onto the bed to straddle this beauty. Hans could see Steven's big dick sliding in and out of Mike's throbbing hole. With one hand, Steven held onto Mike's waist for support, while with his other, he pulled on his own nipples, throwing his head back in ecstasy as he did so. Mike, in the meantime, was working on his own cock, stroking its full length frantically. Through the glass, Hans saw Steven mouth, "I'm coming!" Hans increased his speed. As the first drops of Hans's cum hit the bedroom floor, so Steven let out a cry of pleasure, let go of his nipples, and with both hands, held onto Mike as he pounded away at his ass, filling it with his warm love-juices. Mike met every thrust that Steven made, and in so doing, shot his bolt. Hans saw Mike's white cream shoot from his enormous cock and land on the bed, but it never seemed to stop. As Mike shot, so his ass muscles clamped tightly around Steven's swollen dick, milking every last drop of hot cum from his lover. When both had emptied themselves, Mike collapsed on the bed with Steven, still impaled in him, falling across his back. Steven lay there kissing Mike's neck, ears and back until eventually his limp dick slipped from its warm protective home, and he rolled from Mike's back and lay next to him while they both fell asleep and Hans put his cock away and zipped up his pants.

As Hans exited from the room, Barry's door opened and Hans saw him.

"I wouldn't disturb them if I were you. Steven has just arrived and I think they might be busy for a while," said Hans winking at Barry.

"Oh well, in that case I might as well go for a stroll along the canals," said Barry, walking downstairs with Hans, who was smiling to himself.

Barry made his way along the Prisengracht canal and passed a couple of coffee shops. As he passed the first, he stopped, inhaled, backtracked and inhaled again. A distinct odor of burning marijuana floated through the air. The heady aroma filled his lungs and he smiled to himself. He contemplated going into the coffee shop, but then resisted and headed southwards towards the center of the city. Trams rattled passed him and he had to dodge the numerous bicycles that sped along the narrow cobbled roads.

He soon found himself in what is called the 'Walletjes' or red-light district with its neon-lit windows where the prostitutes parade their wares at night. Being early evening, there wasn't much action but it fascinated Barry to see how they plied their trade. He continued his journey around the city and its cobbled streets until he eventually found himself back at the hotel.

Ascending the stairs from the street entrance, he met Hans in the reception area.

"Sorry to worry you Hans, but tell me, are drugs allowed here in Amsterdam?"

Hans scowled at Barry before answering.

"I hope that you are not thinking of getting into drugs, because if you are, I'll have to deal with you and tell Mike."

"No," laughed Barry, embarrassedly, "it's just that I walked past a coffee shop and I smelt marijuana coming from there."

"Oh!" exclaimed a relieved Hans. "Is that all. Ja, you can smoke cannabis legally in the coffee shops. Any place where you see a picture of palm leaves or perhaps Rastafarian colors will definitely be selling something to do with cannabis."

"Hey, that's awesome," replied Barry, excitedly. "You've actually got more liberating laws here than we have back in the States."

"Well this country has always shown a tolerance to minority groups, and that's why gays, for example, are so happy to be in Amsterdam."

"I think it's good that Holland is. It's a pity more countries aren't like this."

While Hans and Barry were preoccupied in their conversation, Mike and Steven awoke, they showered together and got dressed to go out. Steven poured his lithe body back into his skin-tight leathers, adjusted his balls and cock so that they hung down towards his left leg and pulled on a cropped vest, which revealed his taut stomach muscles apart from his muscular arms and chest. Mike hauled himself into his pair of equally tight leather pants that he'd bought in London, and a T-shirt. Both men looked ready to be raped they looked so gorgeous. They went downstairs to the reception area where Hans was still talking to Barry.

"I see you two beauties have decided to get out of bed and pay us visit," said Hans.

"Hi, Barry," said Steven, hugging the young man to him and kissing him on both cheeks. "It's so good to see you again. Are you well?"

"Fine thanks Steve, and you?"

"Can't you see how happy I am to be here?"

"And I know someone else who's equally happy that you're here," joked Barry, winking at Mike.

"I hope you enjoyed yourself," said Hans to Mike, also winking as he said it.

"What do you mean?" asked Mike, blushing slightly.

"Hmm! He is big," whispered Hans to Mike.

"How do you know?" asked Mike.

Hans merely laughed, but didn't answer Mike's question. "So what are you two lovelies going to do tonight?" asked Hans.

"We thought we'd go out for a meal and then maybe have an early night," said Steven, putting his arm around Mike's waist and giving him a hug. "After all, we have to fly out tomorrow."

"All the more reason why you should have a night out on the town," said Hans. "Why don't you go to one of the leather bars before you go, seeing how you are dressed?"

"I don't think I want any of those guys getting their hands on my man," said Mike. "In any case, we want to be together."

"Oh well, suit yourselves," said Hans. "Of course, you could have a sauna here if you felt like it."

"Do you have a sauna here?" asked Steven, looking a little surprised as most hotels in Amsterdam wouldn't have such a luxury.

"Didn't I tell you?" asked Mike. "It's actually quite nice to have one and then fall straight into bed."

"What do you want to do, Barry?" asked Mike, realizing that now that Steven had arrived, and he was so happy to be with him, he had neglected Barry.

"Hey, you guys go out and enjoy yourselves. I'll just wander around a bit."

This worried Mike because he knew that the last time they went different ways, Barry had landed in trouble and the last thing he wanted now was to lose Barry again.

"Why don't you come and have dinner with us and then if you want to do something, maybe we can do it together or we'll make a plan."

Barry agreed to this and the three got ready to set off.

"Come on Mike," said Steven, "let's go and get something to eat before I die of hunger or fade away."

"You could never fade away," said Mike, taking Steven's hand and leading him out of the hotel foyer into the warm evening air.

The three wandered around the streets of Amsterdam, looking at the passers-by and the buildings. As it was summer, it was still light so many people flocked the streets and the sun still warmed everyone who was about.

"Why don't we go on a dinner cruise?" asked Steven.

"As long as it's only a dinner cruise and no other type of cruising," joked Mike.

They headed towards one of the canals where they found a boat, which offered dinner cruises. They sat down at one of the tables, ordered some champagne and drank a toast to each other and their futures. As the boat sailed smoothly along the canals and under the brightly lit bridges, Mike and Steven sat smiling into each other's eyes and planning their future, while Barry watched the colorfully lit bridges going past, reminiscing about his holiday. When the cruise was over, Mike turned to Steven and said, "What would you like to do now?"

"I think your friend, Hans was right when he said that as it was our last night here we should go out and enjoy ourselves."

"So what do you want to do?"

"Let's go for a drink and take it from there," said Steven. "Would you like to do that, Barry?"

"That sounds great to me. Sure," replied Barry, glad to have been accepted and included in their plans by Steven.

They wandered past a number of quaint pubs until they found one that they liked and entered. The atmosphere was smoky with quite a few people standing at the bar drinking and chatting, while two guys were playing on the pool table. They ordered a couple of beers and stood talking to one another. After a few more drinks, Mike said that he needed the toilet, which was situated up some stairs, so off he went. He was away for a while and Steven wondered what was taking him so long.

"I'm just going to see where Mike is," said Steven, going up the stairs to see where Mike was.

When he reached the landing leading to the toilet, he saw Mike standing next to a doorway.

"Hey, what's been keeping you?" asked Steven.

"Hey Steve, this must be a backroom. When I was in the toilet, I looked in the mirror and I saw the reflection of the doorway and a number of guys going in and out."

"So what do you want to do?" asked Steven.

"Should we go in? But where's Barry?"

"Downstairs. But if we do, you'd better hold my hand, because I don't want to lose you in there," said Steven.

Slowly the two men entered into the darkness, Mike fumbling his way along a wall until he bumped into someone. He felt a hand grasp his crotch.

"Why have you stopped?" whispered Steven.

Mike turned his head to Steven and whispered back, "because, I'm being groped."

Mike felt the zip of his pants being pulled down and a hand slide in and grab hold of his cock. The hand pulled his cock out and then he felt the warm mouth of someone wrap around his length. Mike pulled Steven closer to him and in the direction of where he thought the guy was. The unknown guy was busy getting Mike's cock harder when Steven bumped into him in the dark. The man kept working on Mike's cock but also felt for Steven's. When he found it in Steven's leathers, he ran his hand over its full length. Without removing his mouth from Mike, he shucked Steven's leathers down to the ground and proceeded to stroke Steven's cock. He then removed his mouth from Mike's hard dick and swallowed Steven's.

Steven and Mike stood next to each other having their cocks alternately sucked while they kissed each other. At one stage, the unknown guy tried to take both of their cocks into his mouth at the same time, but owing to their size, he found the act difficult, but it didn't prevent him from trying harder. While Mike and Steven's tongues fought in each other's mouths, so the man's tongue and mouth worked on their dicks until Mike whispered, "I'm coming!"

"So am I," whispered Steven. Both men came at the same moment. As they shot, they could feel the man trying to take both of their cum into his mouth at the same time. When they finished, they zipped up and headed for the light in the doorway and went back downstairs to have another drink together.

"Next time I'm not letting you go to the toilet on your own," said Steven, "because you get us into trouble."

"I wouldn't call that trouble," said Mike, "I'd call that fun, especially when you've got your partner with you."

"Tell me, Mike, would you have gone in if I hadn't come looking for you?"

"Definitely not!" exclaimed Mike, "and that's a promise. Hell I've kept my promises so far, haven't I?"

"What have you two been up to?" asked Barry when they arrived back at their drinks.

"Should we tell him?" questioned Mike.

"I think he's man enough to know," replied Steven.

"If you want a bit of fun, take a walk up to the toilet but go in the doorway that's next to the toilet."

"Why? What's going on there?"

"Just go and you'll find out. That's of course if you want a bit of fun," added Mike.

Barry put down his beer, gave both men one last quizzical look and made his way up the stairs. When he reached the doorway he stopped and peered into the pitch darkness of the room. Slowly Barry made his way into the darkness, feeling along the wall as he moved. He could hear faint breathing noises, but didn't bump into anyone. He went further into the darkness and then suddenly felt a body up against his. A hand reached down to his crotch. He let the hand feel along his slowly growing length. He reciprocated and felt for the other person's crotch, but instead of feeling material of clothing, he felt the warm flesh of a man's erect cock. He could feel from the shape that it was cut and had a large mushroom-shaped head.

Slowly Barry knelt and guided the mushroom-shaped head into his waiting mouth. He could feel the man's cock throb as he closed his young lips around the thick stem, then he began to slide his mouth along its length. The man thrust forward, forcing his cock deeper into Barry's throat, but this never dampened Barry's enthusiasm. The sound of Barry's mouth slurping up and down the man's cock increased and soon other bodies began to muster around them. Barry became aware that other cocks were being thrust in the direction of his mouth. He was tempted to take some others, but he enjoyed the thickness and length of the current recipient of his favors.

The sounds increased in volume and with it, heavy breathing was evident. Soon gasps and groans were heard and Barry could feel wet, sticky cum landing on his shirt and face, but still he kept up his action.

The thrusts into Barry's throat became more frantic and he was aware that the man was about to shoot his load, so Barry prepared for the onslaught. A long, low growl emanated from the man's throat as Barry sank to the base of the man's cock and the first load went straight down Barry's throat. Soon his mouth was filling up with a salty-sweet taste. Barry swallowed as rapidly as he could, but the man held Barry's head and fucked it, shooting load after load. Barry never flinched and it was only when the man's cock was limp that he removed it from Barry's warm mouth.

Barry rose to his feet and headed towards the toilet to clean himself. As he entered the toilet a tall guy of about mid-twenties, with short-cropped brown hair followed him in. The man smiled at Barry and said, "You speak English?"

"Yes," replied Barry, wet cum still trickling down Barry's face.

"You give an awesome blowjob," said the man, going to the urinal and pulling out his semi-hard cock to piss.

"Thanks," answered Barry, "and I think you have the most awesome cock."

The man turned so that Barry could see it once more, but this time in the light. He smiled and thanked Barry for the compliment.

"Are you here alone?" enquired the man.

"No, I'm with some friends."

"Pity, maybe we could have gone back to my place."

Barry was unsure what to do. He knew that Mike and Steven wanted to do their own thing and be together, but he also was fearful of anything untoward happening to him again, so he said, "maybe we could make a plan if they go out and you could come back to my hotel."

"I'd like that. By the way my name is Johan."

"Hi, I'm Barry."

Barry washed his face and cleaned all the evidence from it, dried himself and made his way back down stairs.

"Well, you were quite a long time," said Mike. "Did you manage to have some fun?"

Barry blushed and nodded.

"I can see you had a really good time, said Steven, running a finger over the shoulder of Barry's shirt. "A little evidence is still there."

"Are you two guys going out after we leave here?" asked Barry, trying to change the subject.

"Why, have you got a date?" enquired Mike.

"It depends on you guys. If you want to go somewhere without me, that's OK."

"Who's the date?" asked Mike, surveying the bar.

The man Barry had spoken to in the toilet came down the stairs.

"That guy coming down the stairs," said Barry, pointing Steven and Mike in the right direction.

"Well, at least your nephew's got good taste, Mike."

"Wow, that's a stunner!" exclaimed Mike. "I might even dump Steve to go with that."

"You do that and you're dead," retorted Steven.

"Barry, if you want to go with him, that's fine by me, but you take him back to the hotel and you tell Hans so that he can keep an eye on you. If you're not happy with those arrangements, then you don't go with the guy. By the way, do you know his name?"

"Yes, he said it was Johan."

"Then you invite him over here so I can meet him and offer him a drink," continued Mike.

Barry crossed over to the counter where Johan was standing.

"Hi, Johan would you like to join us for a drink?"

Johan turned and saw Mike and Steven smiling at him.

"Sure, thanks."

The two young men went back to where Mike and Steven were and Barry introduced them to his new friend. They stood around chatting and it was clear to Mike that Johan was truly impressed with Barry.

While they sat together, Mike and Steven enjoyed each other's company, surveying the men coming and going to the bar and commenting on them. Mike had noticed that a number of men had been eyeing Steven in his tight leathers with his bulging crotch, but he wasn't jealous, instead he was proud.

"I don't know whether you're aware that quite a few guys want to take you to bed," said Mike.

Steven looked surprised to hear this. "You're joking, aren't you?"

"No I'm not. You see that short guy with the moustache standing at the far end of the bar, well he's been watching you for some time; and the guy with the jeans at the pool table tries to play every shot looking at you – I'm not surprised that he's losing," said Mike.

"Are you jealous?" asked Steven with a twinkle in his eyes.

"Not at all," said Mike, with authority, "because I know that they can't have you, so they can look as much as they like."

After about another half an hour, the guy who had been playing pool came over to them and asked Steven if he would like a drink. Steven looked at Mike as if to seek advice, but Mike just shrugged his shoulders.

"Thanks, but no thanks," said Steven. "If you want to buy me a drink you'll have to buy my lover one as well," he said, putting his arm around Mike's waist.

The pool player looked at both of them, turned away and headed back to the pool table. Both Mike and Steven burst out laughing at his actions.

"I'm proud of you Steve. You've got the looks and the body, not to mention the dick, to get anyone that you want, but you chose not to get involved with that guy." As he said this, Mike turned to Steven and kissed him passionately on the lips. When their lips parted, Steven said, "Let's go home, Mike."

"Barry, are you and Johan coming along with us? We're going back to the hotel."

Barry looked up at the tall Johan as if to ask whether he wanted to go back to the hotel with Barry. They both nodded.

"Yep, we're coming too."

They walked through the streets of Amsterdam with their arms around each other's shoulders until they reached the hotel.

"Do you feel like a sauna?" asked Mike, as they entered.

"Gee that sounds like a good idea," replied Steven.

The two made their way up to their bedroom, stripped off their clothes, grabbed a couple of towels, wrapped them around their waists and set off for the sauna.

In the meantime, Barry escorted Johan back to his room, where they too stripped very rapidly and settled down on Barry's bed.

When Mike and Steven got to the sauna, they went into its warmth and dropped their towels. They sat on the bench luxuriating in the warmth that abounded around them. After a while Mike stretched out on his back on the bench, putting his head on Steven's crotch. Steven ran his fingers through Mike's hair. As he did so, Mike turned sideways so that his face turned towards Steven's cock. Mike opened his mouth and engulfed Steven's growing cock and gently sucked on it, as a baby might do to a teat. Just as they were beginning to enjoy their pleasures, the door to the sauna opened and in walked Hans. He froze at the sight that greeted him.

"I am terribly sorry to walk in on you two like this, I really didn't expect to find you here."

"Welldon'tstandthereletting thewarmairout, comeinandclosethedoor." Hans entered embarrassedly and closed the door. He went and sat on the bench slightly away from the other two. Mike hadn't stopped working on Steven's dick and continued to slurp up and down its length. Steven was enjoying this, especially as he now had an audience. Hans had removed his towel and Steven could see Hans begin to play with his young cock.

When Mike had sufficiently slicked Steven's cock, he turned to Hans and said, "Do you want a taste of this?"

Hans didn't know what to say at first, but then the temptation of Steven's nine and half inch cock was too much for him. He moved to where Mike had been and knelt in front of Steven's engorged cock, taking it in his mouth to the depths of his throat. Mike, in the meantime had positioned himself in front of Steven so that Steven could suck his big cock. Once Mike felt that his cock was wet enough, he told Steven to stand up. As he did as he was told, Hans let go of Steven's cock and watched to see what was going to happen. Mike turned Steven around and positioned his bargepole at the entrance to Steven's ass. Steven pushed slowly back onto Mike's shaft and Hans saw Mike's ten-inches slide right the way into Steven. As soon as Mike felt Steven's warmth wrap around his cock, he started a slow rhythmic motion and began to fuck Steven. Hans watched with anticipation, stroking his own cock.

"Hans, suck Steven's cock," said Mike.

Hans needed no second invitation and went down on Steven's cock making it as wet as he could.

After a while, Mike said, "Hans, turn around and push that cute ass of yours onto Steven's dick."

Hans couldn't believe his ears, but he did as he was told. He turned his back to Steven and held Steven's cock as he guided it into his pucker. Hans held his breath as Steven's cock inched its way into the warm chute. Once Steven was in him, the three began a gentle rocking motion with Mike fucking Steven who in turn was fucking Hans. The sweat was pouring off them from the heat of the sauna and from the action and their bodies glistened in the light.

Hans worked feverishly on his own dick and could feel himself getting closer to coming.

"I'm getting close!" he exclaimed.

"Come Hans. Ride that dick of mine," said Steven.

"Oooh! Fuck my ass!" screamed Hans as he shot a load onto the sauna floor.

"Aargh! Tighten that ass on my cock. Fuck this cock," shouted Steven as he rammed into Hans. As he did this, so his butt slid deeper onto Mike's cock.

"Work my ass, Mike," shouted Steven. "Fuck this ass with that big dick! Deeper! Harder, Mike!"

Mike obliged and was breathing heavily from the feeling that Steven's ass was creating on his cock.

"Steve, I'm coming!" exclaimed Mike, and he pounded into Steven's ass.

Hans was still impaled on Steven's cock, tightening his ass muscles and creating pressure on Steven's dick.

"Aaargh!" cried Steven as he shot into Hans. "Oh yes! Oh that's good! Come on Mike!"

Mike let out a roar and flooded Steven's ass with his hot cum. He groaned and grunted as he pounded into Steven, filling him with all the love that he had. His actions were so intense that poor Hans was sent forward onto the bench having released his clutch on Steven's dick. Hans sat on the bench as he watched Mike impaling Steven as the two of them kissed passionately. Steven put his arms around the back of Mike, holding onto him so that he couldn't pull out.

"Stay there, don't pull out," gasped Steven, as his cock throbbed in the air.

Hans could see Steven's ass muscles tighten and then relax as he tried to get Mike's cock to shoot again. Slowly Steven started riding Mike's length again, pushing forwards and backwards. Hans could see its full length penetrating into the dark depths of Steven and then slowly retreat towards the daylight. He felt his own cock coming back to life again, watching the two young men at it.

Mike, still inside Steven, moved towards the bench and sat down taking Steven with him. Once he was seated, Steven began riding Mike's cock down to its base. Hans moved to between their legs so that he could view Mike's fucking better. Steven rose and fell on that long shaft, taking its full length and groaning with pleasure as he did so. Hans licked his fingers and as Steven rose on Mike's cock, Hans inserted two fingers along the ridge of Mike's cock. When Steven fell on Mike's cock, he felt the extra pressure of having a cock and two fingers up his ass. The pressure built up in both Mike and Steven and they were being turned on by Hans's action. Steven writhed in pleasure trying to get Mike's balls and more inside of him, until he exploded and shot his hot, white cum up into the air, landing on his tight belly and running down the length of his cock. At the same moment, Mike gave a sharp upward thrust and emptied another load of love into Steven's guts. Mike collapsed against the wall of the sauna and Steven collapsed against Mike's chest, both panting from exhaustion. Once the three of them had recovered, they all went to Mike and Steven's room to shower and clean up.

Meanwhile in Barry's room, the young American had spent most of his time, enjoying the thick mushroom-shaped head of Johan's long cock that he had so enjoyed earlier. Johan had positioned the young, lithesome American's trim body on the bed, lifted his legs high into the air and aimed his long cock at Barry's quivering opening.

"Please be gentle, Johan," whispered Barry as the Dutch hunk neared him.

As the head of Johan's cock touched Barry, he tensed.

Johan could see fear in Barry's eyes.

"Are you OK with me doing this to you?" asked Johan, calmly.

"Yes," replied Barry, "but no one as big as you has ever screwed me before."

Johan smiled, leaned forward and kissed Barry on the forehead.

"I promise I'll go slow and be gentle with you, and if I hurt you, you must tell me and I'll stop. OK?"

Barry smiled back and nodded.

Slowly Johan pushed forward and slowly he entered Barry, then he would withdraw until Barry became used to Johan's size.

Eventually, Johan sank deep into Barry and the young man sighed and smiled up at the hunk towering over him.

"Are you OK?" asked Johan.

"Now I am," replied Barry.

Their love-making was long and slow with Johan allowing Barry to dictate the speed and depth of penetration, but when they both climaxed together, Barry felt a sensation he had never experienced before.

As they came down from their high, Barry couldn't stop praising and thanking Johan for his care and gentleness. They lay in each other's arms for some time before either of them spoke.

"How was that Barry?"

"Beautiful," was the answer.

Back in Mike's room, he and Steven showered and then sat on the bed while Hans sat on one of the chairs.

"You are a very lucky person, Mike having someone like Steven," said Hans.

"You said something to me when Steven first arrived at the hotel; how did you know?" asked Mike.

"Know what?" asked Hans.

"You said that Steven was big. How did you know because that was the first time you had met him?"

Hans roared with laughter. "You're going to kill me," he said.

"Why?" asked Mike.

"Steven, do you mind if I borrow Mike just for a minute?"

"Sure," replied Steven, "but I don't know what you two are up to."

Hans took Mike out of his room and lead him into the room next door. When they went in, Mike saw a 'window' and couldn't believe his eyes when he looked into it – there sat Steven.

Mike was ready to kill Hans when he realized that it was a one-way mirror.

"You mean you watched us having sex!" exclaimed Mike.

"I'm afraid so, but hell, it was good," said Hans. "Will you forgive me?"

Mike glared at him and then smiled. "Of course, provided you enjoyed watching."

The two then went back to Steven in the other room and told him what Hans had done. Steven saw the funny side to it and, being a stripper, he enjoyed performing in front of other people.

Hans then bade them a good night and left their room, leaving Steven and Mike to climb into bed and wrap their arms around each other and fall into a happy, contented sleep.

In room 16, Barry and Johan spent the entire night either cuddled up together in each other's arms, or making love to each other.

The following day Johan said his farewell to Barry while in the other room, Mike and Steven packed their luggage.

The three young men went down for breakfast and both Mike and Steven were eager to find out about Barry's night.

"Come on, tell us all," demanded Mike. "You know everything I do, so now I have to know everything that you get up to."

"Did Johan stay the night?" asked Steven.

Barry looked confidently at both men and smiled at them.

"Yes!"

"Well, that's a good start," remarked Steven to Mike.

"And...?" said Mike, trying to eek out of his nephew some juicy details.

"We had sex," answered Barry.

"And ...?" taunted Mike.

Barry hesitated.

"Come on!" exclaimed Steven. "You're driving us crazy with anticipation.

"He made beautiful love to me."

"He fucked you!" cheered Mike.

Barry nodded, blushing as he did so.

"And ...?"

"And I enjoyed it," replied Barry.

Both Mike and Steven hugged Barry to their chests, smothering him with kisses.

"You've really come of age, Barry," said Mike when he'd finished almost suffocating his young nephew with affection.

"What's going on here?" asked Hans as he entered on the scene.

Mike excitedly told Hans that, "Barry's had his first proper fuck!"

The jollification and cheering from the three older men was something out of this world. Barry thought he was in some fantasy world with the euphoria that abounded around him.

"Hey guys, anyone would think I'd given birth or something," said Barry, trying to calm them down.

"Well in nine months time you might find yourself pregnant," joked Steven.

"True," echoed Mike, "but at least we know who the father is."

"And that would mean we'd have to come back to Amsterdam to show the father the baby, wouldn't we?" jested Steven.

"Cut it out guys. Anyone would think it was the first time I'd ever had sex," quipped Barry, trying to get them to stop joking with him.

"You might have had sex before, but this is different," said Mike, softly, "this is special as it's the first time you've done it properly with a guy, and I'm proud of you."

Mike hugged Barry to him, kissing him tenderly.

"You know how much I love you."

"Yes, I do, Mike. And thank you for everything. I owe so much to you and your love and friendship. Steven, you don't know what a magnificent man you've got yourself," said Barry, pulling Steven in to join his and Mike's hugs.

When Hans had decided that he'd seen enough passion for an early morning, he interrupted their camaraderie.

"Hey guys, you've got to get to the airport. Come on let's get you packed into the car and head off."

Hans took them to the airport to catch their flight home, and there they exchanged addresses and kissed each other good-bye.

"Thanks for a wonderful time, Hans. Next time we come overseas, we'll spend more time here in Amsterdam with you, that's a promise," said Mike.

"You'd better, and you had better look after this gorgeous man of yours, because if you don't, I'm going to take him for myself," joked Hans.

"Don't worry, Hans, nobody is going to get into this young hunk except me," smiled Mike putting an arm around Steven as though to protect him.

"And nobody's going to get this man of mine," said Steven. "Thanks for a lovely time, Hans; and I hope to see you again. Listen, if you ever want to visit us, just give us a call and you're welcome to stay with us."

"I'll echo that," said Mike. "Well, buddy, I think we'd better get going."

Barry hugged Hans and thanked him for the wonderful time he'd had in Amsterdam.

"I'm sorry that I couldn't get to give you some special treatment, Barry, but maybe next time."

"That's a promise. Next time we visit you in Amsterdam, my first night is with you and you can show me another side to Amsterdam," replied Barry.

They hugged and kissed each other and Mike, Steven and Barry vanished through the customs area to board their flight.

As the KLM flight lifted into the sky, it circled over Amsterdam, almost like a final salute, headed off towards the Atlantic Ocean and the three guys settled back to start new and exciting lives together.

About the Author

Lew Bull, who lives in Johannesburg, South Africa, has been published in a number of anthologies including, among others, *Ultimate Gay Erotica 2007* and *2008, Treasure Trail, Fast Balls, Travelrotica and Travelrotica Vol. 2, Don't Ask, Don't Tie Me Up, Cruise Lines* and *My First Time Vol. 5.*

Although he is involved in education, and has a Doctorate in this field, it is writing and traveling that brings him most pleasure.

Lew Bull is also the author of ***Power Buddies***. Available at your local bookstore, Amazon.com or TheNazcaPlainsCorp.com

www.ingramcontent.com/pod-product-compliance
Lightning Source LLC
Chambersburg PA
CBHW070757280626
47162CB00016B/1417